Move Over James Bond
and Other Stories

Vera Mary Murray

Copyright © 2009, 2019 Veronica (Vera) Mary Murray

All rights reserved. No part of this book may be reproduced, stored in a retrieval system or transmitted in any form or by any means without the prior written permission of the publisher, nor be otherwise circulated in any form of binding or cover other than that In which it is published and without a similar condition being imposed on the subsequent purchaser.

First published in Australia in 2009, by Bent Banana Books, 24 Lorraine Court, LAWNTON. QLD, AUSTRALIA 4501. This reprint, 2019

PUBLISHER - BENT BANANA BOOKS

ILLUSTRATIONS:
Cover sketches by Ben Croyden and Claire Croyden

First edition
A CiP Catalogue record for this book is available from the Australian National Library.
ISBN   -   9780980568417

Photo on front cover by Joanne Croyden
Typeset in Garamond 12pt

CONTENTS

Move over James Bond: Assignment 1	4
Trapped	12
Lexie's ghost	18
Two shades of murder	19
Footsteps in the night	22
Cry on the wind	30
Cheeky Charlie meets his match	38
In the nick of time	39
Beyond the Black Stump	41
Yesterday's Santa	44
Your mother has to go	49
Marcia's trip to Mars: Year 2055	52
Move over James Bond: Assignment 2	56
When the worst comes to the worst	67
Wages of sin	70
The end of Peggy-Dan.	77
A bloke can be real unlucky	79
1945	83
Godfrey smells a rat	91
Move over James Bond: Assignment 3	94
His own man	101
Love bounces	103
Love is like the measles	108
The second Adam	109
Was it black?	131
Child needs a paddling	134
Toby to the rescue	127
Get a life	135
Letter of destiny	138
The other woman	145
A revolving door	150
Shadow in the mist of memory	153
His last good deed	172

MOVE OVER JAMES BOND; ASSIGNMENT 1

AT 6:45AM, ERNEST JONES (now using his newly acquired surname Moneylove) undercover drug enforcement officer and devotee of James Bond, 007, that famous suave spy of film fame with authority to shoot to kill, scrunched down between the two hibiscus bushes on the curb close to Bernice Wong's store. He stayed poised and mentally alert despite the irritation where the rough seams of his brand new khaki overalls, dragged and abraded along his inner thighs each time he tucked his legs closer to his body. *Should have washed them*, he conceded to himself. *Roughed them up a bit, dirtied them. It's hard to look like a tradesman squatting on the kerb waiting for a lift to work, in brand new clobber.*

He casually glanced around at Bernice's store and his nose twitched at the sight of bulging rubbish bins, piles of discarded containers, and stacks of disused boxes scattered about the property at the side of the shop. *Ahh…a good place to hide drugs. As soon as Bernice makes a wrong move and leads me to them, it's on to rounding up the main player, and another step towards James Bond spy status, ahead of Smithy, the rotten crawler.*

His began to relive the time he was summoned to the office of Mr Grant Stand, his Chief Executive Officer. 'I know you're keen to move up the ranks in surveillance Moneylove, and the Drug Squad always values conscientiousness.' Ernest had beamed. 'Smithy's out on a secret mission so I'm giving you an undercover job… and this time don't blow it.'

'I won't, Thank you sir.'

'To fill you in…several Asians who arrived in the country recently have been arrested on drug smuggling charges. Unfortunately this puts everyone on the same flight under suspicion. One of them, a Soonee Wong on a temporary visa is staying with his Aunt Bernice. She sells groceries, drinks, Chinese herbs and remedies. Your assignment is to keep a watch on them. But remember, we're after the big guy." The C.E.O. had then fixed him with his eyes narrowed. "Reckon you could handle it Ernest? It's the sort of thing careers can build on, so

don't foul up this time.'

Moneylove recalled the delightful wrench in his gut as the C.E.O. for the first time had called him by his first name. He wondered if Smithy, the 'favourite' was on such close terms with the chief, but doubted it. Smithy might get the best assignments, but this time he would prove he was a class higher. He straightened his shoulders and lifted his chin higher.

'I won't sir. Thank you sir.' Ernest's wide grin had threatened to attack his ears as he tried to look Cool, Confident, and Capable; the three C's his C.E.O. claimed were the hallmarks of his officers' success. Ernest had no doubts he himself was cool, confident and capable. He would land Mr. Big Guy. It was 'in the bag' so to speak.

'What procedure do you have in mind sir?'

'For you... a tradesman waiting outside the shop for a lift to work, and then dropped off there again at night. You keep a low profile and note anything suspicious. Keep us informed of regular customers and anyone you have doubts about. Mick Carbello who's got the fish shop across the road is your local contact if you need one. He says Bernice appears worried. Her nephew's rarely seen. He bunks down in a back room at the shop apparently, but Bernice lives elsewhere and arrives about 7am to open up, and....'

Ernest had stopped listening. His eyes glazed over as he planned his strategy – *6.45am set up position; 8.30, a second-hand Holden (not to arouse suspicion) drug squad car would pick me up. Then back again at 5.30.*

Ernest's mental drift back to the past was aborted by the encroaching clip clop of Bernice's sandals. He held the open book that he had cleverly thought to bring, and covered the lower part of his face with it. He watched her enter the store through the side door. A few moments later she re-appeared carrying a box of empty bottles. She deposited them on the ground beside the steps before going back inside.

Alert for her regular early morning visitor described to him by Carbello, Ernest had not long to wait. A lean, clean-cut, khaki-clad rider bumped his pushbike up over the gutter, and dismounted after entering Bernice's yard. He gathered up the discarded bottles and placed them in a basket on the handlebars of his bike. He usually hurried away, Carbello had said, but not this morning. He kept standing beside his bike, obviously waiting to see Bernice.

He doesn't fool me, dressed like a tradesman in new khaki overalls – an active participant in the drug scene no doubt.

Bernice re-appeared and handed him a white plastic bag. Ernest turned his head and leaned sideways in order to hear what was being said.

"Maurice, guard it well. It's getting more difficult to get the powder into Australia. Now, make sure Mr. Sing pays up. He's a bit forgetful. His other order hasn't arrived yet so if you don't meet the courier on the way tell Mr Sing to expect it tomorrow."

"I'll pick up my supply then too."

She pressed money into his hand. "Call this a donation.'

The man mumbled something Ernest did not grasp. He almost jumped for joy. *At last… I've hit the jackpot. Can't wait to see Smithy's face when I get that promotion.* Rippling with the thrill of it all Ernest drew out his mobile phone. He quickly dialled through to the squad car driver, waiting in readiness.

"Follow the man in khaki on the push-bike. He's just turned into North Street. He's delivering. Pick me up after you've nabbed him handing over the goods and collecting the money."

"Sure Ernest. We're on our way."

Ernest jumped to his feet. It was time to move. Staying past his pick-up time would only raise suspicion. He forced himself to walk nonchalantly with the intention of crossing the street to Carbello's, from where he would ring his boss in private.

Suddenly his path was blocked by a middle-aged buxom woman with very short frizzy hair, who had somehow bounced around from behind to block his path. Her wide nose was flat – glued to a pockmarked face that looked as if it had been through a few bouts with the champion American boxer Muhammad Ali. From beneath heavy drooping eyelids, the woman was staring at his clothes – his body? He felt alarmed that he had not seen her before, or heard her creep up on him. *Very un-James Bond of me.*

"The boss said you'd be wearing khaki," she lisped through protruding well-spaced teeth.

Trained to listen and encourage eager lips he agreed. "You're right. I am wearing khaki." *And so was the bike-rider. This must be the courier.*

"I've got the order."

This is better than I dreamed. "Thanks, but I'm the new kid on the block so who do I thank?"

"Mr Ling Wei Fu, Importer. I think this stuff's some of his overseas junk."

"And you are?"

"Ethelynn," she shyly mouthed.

"You're his secretary?" *Flattery always helps.*

She giggled. "Nooo, I'm his domestic help. He sent me he says, 'cause I'm an adventurous spirit. He's right...I think...but I ain't had no adventures yet."

"I AM surprised," was Ernest's aside as he noticed the squad car entering the street. Ethelynn seemed pleased.

"So what have you got for me?" he asked.

Ethelynn plunged her plump hand into the depth of her handbag and drew out a packet, which she handed to Ernest.

His fingers prodded its contents from the outside. It was lumpy. *New method...but I'm up to their tricks. It's so you won't feel the powder.* He pocketed it as the office car came to a stop beside them. The two men in the front nodded and winked at Ernest. He nodded back.

He turned to Ethelynn. "We'll give you a lift back to your job Ethelynn, but we'll have to stop at the office first."

Giggling, Ethelynn managed to snort, "Ta."

Her large bulk began to press against him as she squeezed past to enter the back seat of the car, causing her almost football-sized bosom to slap against him. He quivered. *How is it James Bond gets all the beautiful, sexy young woman and I get this blot on womanhood.* Reluctantly he followed her. He seated himself as far as possible away from her, but she kept wriggling closer until her large hot leg scorched his. He was trapped. He tried to direct his mind elsewhere. "Everything go well Siggie?" he enquired of the driver.

"Sure, we nabbed him in the act of handing over the packet and taking money off some old geezer. We got 'em both. Dropped 'em off at headquarters."

The other man cast his eyes in Ethelynn's direction. "Who's that?"

"Mr Big Guy's courier."

"The Big Fella couldn't have picked a better one. Never suspect her. Good work Ernest. The boss'll be pleased."

Ernest found it impossible to wallow in self-appreciation and self-praise. All his efforts were put into trying desperately to wriggle further away, to avoid suffocation from Ethelynn's hot garlic breath and warm throbbing body. It was to no avail. Sweat now glistened on his forehead. He tried to appear interested in the street outside but she insisted on talking. "Mr. Ling's got lots of friends like youse."

"I don't think 'friends' is the right word," he muttered. He then lapsed into silence as he became aware Ethelynn was again running her questing eyes over his body. He shuddered. "Can't you drive faster?" suddenly demanded the now frantic Ernest.

Before the car had completely stopped in the office car park Ernest was out of the vehicle. He rushed into the main office and handed the packet to the C.E.O.'s secretary, requesting immediate attention by the C.E.O.

He was breathing heavily with excitement, anticipating a 'pat on the back' in the form of a promotion, and later a martini 'shaken not stirred.' as James Bond liked it, when he was eventually summoned into Mr. Grant Stand's office. *Move over James Bond. I'm about to share the top spot with you.* As he bounced into the Chief's office he could not control his excitement. "Good job I did, hey boss?" he announced.

The C.E.O.'s eyes narrowed, adding more gloom to his grim expression. Ernest's face drooped in response. He began to think that James Bond would have to wait longer for him.

"Good job?" Mr. Grant Stand raised his voice. "Good job! I should bill you for the time wasted… the embarrassment caused."

"But... but...." sputtered Ernest.

The C.E.O. bent his body forward and spoke slowly as if to a small child. "Your drug courier turned out to be a Maurice Goodfellow, a good-deed-a-day Boy Scout leader who picks up items, mostly bottles, for his group's fund-raising. He bike-rides to save the environment or something."

He then waved an opened paper bag in front of Ernest's face before turning it upside down. White powder spilt on to the desk. "This is what you had the troops pick up at Mr Sing's. Do you know what this is?"

"Dope of some sort...heroin?" he hopefully managed to whisper.

"Rare powdered deer horn...a supposed medicine for virility." Ernest looked puzzled.

"In the sexual area you fool. Once a month this Boy Scout fellow picks up the deer horn powder Bernice Wong imports, along with ginseng for himself and Mr Sing. They both swear deer horn is the tops for one's sex life."

Moneylove felt embarrassed and hated it...not a James Bond thing. "But..." he sputtered, hopefully attempting to redeem himself. "The bike-rider could have gone into the shop for deer horn powder. Why the back door business?"

The C.E.O. sighed deeply. "Because it's quicker to have it ready for him I suppose. And as for this." The chief upturned the bag from Ethelynn. Dried roots tumbled out." Ernest gasped. There was no powder, and the roots did not look like what the manual claimed any drug looked like. *Perhaps they've been hollowed out. Those drug barons are smart.*

His boss read his bewildered expression. "These are ginseng roots you idiot." shouted the C.E.O. "They claim that ginseng gives you extra strength. They also claim that taking both Ginseng and deer horn powder is the best combination since butter joined bread."

Ernest slid slowly into the chair opposite his chief. His expectations were vanishing; his dreams dissolving, but he struggled on. "But...but...Bernice? What about those mysterious visits Carbello says she's been making to the city?"

"To the Department of Immigration to get an extension of her nephew's visa."

The C.E.O. leaned closer to Ernest and became more intense. "Fortunately, we checked up on your ...err...investigation results, and thanks to Smithy, we found that what you managed to obtain in the way of evidence of a drug ring were two items both legal in this country. If I had gone ahead with this I would have been laughed out of the Organisation.

Ernest cringed as his boss, now red in the face, shouted. "Moneylove, <u>always</u> make sure of your facts or call in your betters. Lift your game!" His voice then dropped to a whisper. "Remember...we still have vacancies in Antarctica."

"Sorry sir. I'll do better next time." Ernest rose quickly to his feet. *Even James Bond had his mishaps, but not for long.*

"Next time! Next time! Oh yes, I do have a job for you. It's...."

"Oh thank you sir for giving me another chance. I'll catch 'em this time." *I'll show that crawler Smithy.*

The C.E.O. gave a forced sideways grin of pleasure. "This job is to deliver that crazy, non-stop giggling Ethelynn back to wherever she came from. Her exuberance over her 'big adventure' as she calls it is driving us insane." Ernest's mouth gaped open in horror.

"Now get on with it!"

Ernest knocked his knee against the chair as he scrambled to escape. Limping through the door and into the passageway, Ernest's stomach turned in a sickening roll as he was immediately confronted with Ethelynn's uninviting and grinning countenance. However, for a brief moment of fascination Ernest watched her tight black curls bounce like demented springs over her skull as she jerked her head up and down in greeting. He groaned as she came closer and backed quickly away.

'I'm to drop you off home." He almost choked on the words.

"That'll be ni-ice." She gazed at him from heavy-hooded eyes as both hands reached out to encompass him. He recoiled, shocked as the realisation dawned. *Hell, she likes me.* The horror of being crushed in a bear hug by Ethelynn caused him to quickly brush past her, foiling any attempt by her to touch him. She followed so close behind he fancied he could feel her hot breath on the back of his neck. He increased his pace; fearful she might fall forward and crush him to death.

I wonder how I can get her to sit in the back seat while I drive? Tell her I've got something contagious? Rabies? AIDS? Hell! James Bond never had problems like this.

Meanwhile, still in his office the Chief was grinning widely as he moved away from his half-opened door after watching Ethe-lynn's bumbling attempts at seducing Ernest.

"There's some satisfaction to be got in this job at times," he muttered.

On resuming his seat at his desk, he reached for the deer horn powder and as an after-thought also pocketed the ginseng. *My wife's in for a treat...or two. I'll be the new man she's been wanting for a long time. Come to think of it that bumbling Moneylove turns out useful at times.*

TRAPPED

THE EVENTS OF SEPTEMBER 11 when terrorist controlled planes brought down the New York Trade Centre, followed by the Bali nightclub bombing, had increased Belinda's fear of flying. When her employer Mr Carney assigned her to visit Bali to buy fabrics for the summer collection of garments at his store, she felt overwhelmed.

"Couldn't you find someone else? It's not safe. Look what's been happening overseas. The very thought of flying makes me very nervous especially after the Wall Street disaster, and the Bali nightclub bombing!"

"That's all past history Belinda, and businesses have to keep going regardless. Face the lion and you'll find it's a pussycat. Give it a go. I thought you'd be pleased. Many young women would give their eye-teeth to get a trip overseas at no cost to themselves. Please…the business needs more stock. I'd send someone else but you're the expert on batik."

This Belinda doubted, but looking at her boss' gloomy expression she thought, 'Perhaps he's right. I should face my fear.' She clasped her hands tightly together as she said, "Okay, I'll go, but if I don't come back, promise me that you'll look after my cat?"

Mr Carney's expression changed to satisfaction. "You have my word, but you'll be back on schedule. Now go home and pack."

"Yes Mr Carney," she said dutifully.

Once on a plane in mid-air Belinda refused to look out the windows and clutched her handbag tightly. She did not undo the safety belt, and when instructions were given on what to do if a disaster happened, she tried not to listen, giving a silent prayer that they would arrive in Denpasar safely.

She had carefully noted the tall, swarthy gentleman when he had moved into the seat next to her. Apart from a small smile, she had avoided making any acknowledgment of him. She was afraid he might have a Middle-Eastern accent. When dinner was served he ordered wine and Belinda felt reassured. *A wine drinker*

– he's unlikely to be a terrorist, or Muslim suicide bomber.

Without warning the plane lurched. The man's half-filled glass pitched sideways and deposited its contents over the front of her dress and on to her lap.

"Oops, sorry. We seem to have hit a pothole," he joked, in an accent she guessed could be Indonesian.

His apologetic manner calmed her fears, until he tried to mop up the moisture with a large handkerchief. Alarmed, Belinda scrambled from her seat and hurried to the ladies rest-room where she attempted to sponge away the red patches, pleased she was wearing silk, which stopped the wine from penetrating to her skin. When she returned to her seat the stain was barely visible.

"I'm so sorry. I didn't mean to alarm you. I was trying to help."

Typical male.

Obviously to Belinda, to make up for the unfortunate mishap, he began to chatter and soon, against her will, Belinda warmed to him. He was charming and his eyes danced as he asked, "May I ask your name?" His broad smile was reassuring.

"Belinda Andrews."

"I am Bruno Franco." His smile remained. Belinda relaxed and forgot her fears as they continued to chat light-heartedly. When she explained her purpose in travelling to Bali, Bruno's smile became even broader.

Before their arrival at Denpasar airport there came the usual instructions to fasten seat belts. Her companion was not in his seat, and she felt an unexpected concern. A few minutes later Bruno returned clutching a box. He seated himself and clicked his seat belt into place.

The plane descended and was braking to a sudden bumpy stop on protesting wheels when he offered her the box. "These chocolates are an attempt to make up for my dreadful behaviour."

"You don't have to," insisted Belinda.

"Please." The pleading tone was too much. She took them. "Thank you."

"Where are you staying?"

"The Eastern Star Hotel."

"So am I. What a strange coincidence. How are you getting there?"

"Taxi."

"How about that? Mind if I share your transport?"

"Not at all," Belinda replied, secretly pleased.

She lost sight of him at the customs line-up, but while her bags were being processed, she noticed him waiting near the exit. Belinda, eager to get on her way was becoming impatient by the time her turn came. The local police were everywhere with their search dogs, and to Belinda's surprise, she saw one of the dogs stop to sniff at her cabin bag. The dog's handler hauled the bag away. "Would you please come this way Miss Andrews?"

"Why? I haven't done anything wrong." She was indignant.

She was taken to large office in a building adjoining the terminal and watched while her bags' contents were scattered over a low table. The dog suddenly leapt up and placed his paw on the box of chocolates Bruno had given her. The official opened it, broke open one of the chocolates and white power fell out.

"Cocaine!" he announced triumphantly.

"Drugs!" Belinda raised her voice in disbelief. "I was given that box by a Mr. Bruno Franco. He said he would be staying at the Eastern Star Hotel."

"Ah, she has an accomplice."

Belinda sank into a chair. *This can't be happening.* The policeman dialled a number. After some conversation he said, "No Bruno Franco registered at that hotel, and no booking. You're under arrest. To bring drugs into our country, serious offence, but if you say they're for your own personal use it go better for you – a fine perhaps."

"I won't. I don't touch the stuff."

The Chief looked at his officer and raised his eyebrows. "We hear that many many times." He sighed. "Then we must keep you here – investigate."

Belinda kept protesting as the officer took her arm and guided her down a hallway and through a large door into an adjoining wing of the building. He stopped and tapped a key against a door. "Prisoner!" he called out.

"Come in," a voice responded. The door swung open and Belinda was prodded through a large room and along a narrow passageway. Her escort then waved her through a door and into a cell-like room containing a wooden bench, bedding and a toilet.

Before her escort could retreat she demanded, "I want to ring the Australian Consul and my employer at home."

"For overseas phone calls, 20,000 rupiahs."

"You know how to charge."

The man shrugged. "Times hard. Everything cost much."

'Okay." Belinda would have given her soul to escape what she suspected lay ahead. She had read of others trapped in filthy gaols in eastern countries for years. She rummaged in her handbag which she was pleased had not been taken away. "Here..."

The man gave a quick look around as he grabbed the notes from her hand and shoved them into his inside pocket. "Come."

Belinda was led along a side passage to a small storage area, and handed the telephone. She immediately rang her employer. "I've been arrested for carrying drugs." Belinda sobbed.

"How can that be possible? It's a horrible mistake. They'll find out and let you go."

"I'm afraid there's more to it than that," Belinda sniffled.

"I'll get on to the Australian Consul. He's sort of a friend. I've met him at several international trade fairs."

A second man entered the room. The one guarding Belinda suddenly jerked the phone from her hand and dropped it on to its cradle. "All finish." The newcomer asked him questions in what Belinda assumed was the local language. Her guard seemed a bit shamefaced when responding. She wondered if he would have to part with part or all of the money she had given him.

Belinda was taken back to her cell. Food was brought in later that night and the next day, but she could not stomach it. It was strange and her stomach was in a knot. She desperately hoped that her boss had made contact with someone who could get her out. She felt she would die in this place if she had to stay another night, but that day and the following one passed and nothing eventuated. Belinda was filled with the fear of rotting in goal far away from home, and she sobbed.

The following morning her previous escort opened the door and called, "You come." Belinda was only too eager to oblige. She was taken to the same office she had passed through on arrival. There were two men seated in front of the large wooden desk with their superintendent behind it. As she entered the two men turned towards her. Belinda rejoiced. She recognised Bruno Franco, but was puzzled as to why he was wearing the same uniform as the others, and not a prisoner like herself, but dismissed the worry. *Now all will be explained.* "Bruno, tell them."

"You make mistake. I am Sergeant Montano." There was a glint in his eyes that Belinda read as amusement. "The Australian Consul has contacted us and it seems that your story must be true. You have good references. We think we will find this Bruno Franco and catch him. You can go. But, first you must settle your debt."

"Debt? What debt?"

The man behind the counter read from a slip of paper in his hand. 'Your stay come to $500.00 in Australian money."

"$500? That's day-light robbery!"

"Many rich friends."

Belinda was desperate to leave. She opened her bag and drew out the money in traveller cheques. It was money she was to use to purchase merchandise. She did not care. That was her boss's problem. He had talked her into coming to Bali. She thrust them into his hand, quickly signed the papers placed in front of her, and almost ran out the door and into the street.

'The only flying I'll be doing from now on is on the plane home. It'll be a breeze compared to what I've been through, and if my boss ever suggests I leave Aussie shores again I'll throttle him,' she vowed.

Back in the room the men laughed as the money was divided between them. "You get promotion Bruno…you very clever. Where you put drug this time?"

"Pushed some under the lining inside the box, and replaced

three chocolates with the drug inside. They're the ones in the red wrapping...the only red ones in the box. One was broken open by my friend in customs." They then shared the chocolates, except for those wrapped in red paper.

Outside, Belinda hailed the closest taxi. "To the airport, " she told the driver. "and HURRY!"

LEXIE'S GHOST

LEXIE claimed she saw a ghost at night in the garden.
They said she was mad.
Her husband was suspicious,
and no amount of searching found a ghost.
Lexie got even more distressed,
claiming it came into their bedroom.
Her husband was a deep sleeper
so, he saw nothing.
Sometimes she woke to find herself outside.
She often found leaves caught in her hair.
With much persuading, her husband agreed
she needed to get away.
She returned after several months,
a boyfriend in tow.
He resembled her description of the ghost.
Lexie was prepared to tell her husband
she loved him still,
but that she needed something more.
But, her husband was gone.
He'd left her a note.
"Lexie darling, I too saw a ghost
turned out to be a woman.
She's taking me back
into her world with her.
I may return, but then again...."

TWO SHADES OF MURDER

THE ROOM IS HALF LIT by the rising moon. The night is still. No sound comes from the garden beyond the open window. The silence is heavy, perhaps in mourning, perhaps in expectancy as it awaits my next move.

The body of my regular supplier of the drugs I crave, lies in a crumpled heap at my feet. The steel handle of my knife glistens as it protrudes from his bleeding chest. A stray accusing moonbeam momentarily entrapped, jumps away – escapes – to settle elsewhere. His bulging eyes stare at me from his contorted face. His mouth sags open. His chins are lost in shadow.

I've killed him! I killed him!

The words form in the seemingly choking air of the half-lit room. The fateful result of the accomplished idea swims before my eyes.

Staggering back against the wall I brace myself with blood-covered hands. All around me is deadly quiet – all but for the incessant pounding of my heart. I gaze now with vague detachment at the body lying in a ridiculously twisted position on the floor.

Report me as a junkie to the police? Have me arrested? Lock me up? Me, Noreen, once his full-time lover! Never!

His flabby face now lies half in, half out, of the darkness. The whole room itself is zebraed in shadow and rays of ghastly white moonlight. In one luminous strip his unblinking vigilant eyes glare with hot resentment it seems, right into my soul, but there are no thoughts behind those sightless eyes, no real resentment either. He is dead! I know. I killed him!

The deflated bag-like pockets beneath his eyes are vaguely discernible, but the lower part of his face is still lost in gloom, and form but a minute part of that repulsive bulk of dead human flesh. I cannot drag my gaze away from that Frankenstein face, nor do I want to. Sudden vengeful joy vibrates through my being. I would do it again just to see him at my feet in death. I feel no pity. I have no penitence. I am merely an observer. My mind seems to have left me, and is watching the whole scenario with untroubled interest, from the deeper blackness suspended above my head. I shut my eyes.

I cannot remember when that sublimely fantastic – at the time also fascinating – idea had been born and grew within my brain. Perhaps it was when, with rebellious anger drowning out jealous rage, I begged him. 'A few drugs, only a few. I'd pay you later. I have no money at the moment.' He refused. How dare he thinks he knows what's right for me.

'A term in jail will be the best for you, before you overdose and kill yourself. No, sorry, you can't move in here but if you agree, I'll arrange for you go into rehab,' he had said. The words had marched like army boots across my mind. Was that hours ago? Was this bitter memory part of this same day, this same life? But then the sun had shone. The world had been alive. Now it lies in death, encircling the gruesome object at my feet.

I have only a vague idea of having come here. My mind failed to register details after that first, or was it the last hit, that gave me a feeling of great courage! Drugs have never given me such a high as they did today. Today I mixed them, but tonight I am desperate for more, and I have no money to buy them. The street dealer was right, more and stronger is better, for never have they given me such an astute mind, or such a sense of purpose. Pete would say I had overdosed…the fool!

The room, still half washed with hollow half-light, seems stuck fast in motionless time. All is electric, eerie. Still no sound drifts in from the garden. My now focused mind astounds me with its clarity of thought. My lips curl in vengeful joy as I study the whole scene. The silence is heavier now. With grief? With breathless anticipation? It is like viewing the setting for a stage play – the shadows, the pressing silence – the possible audience in the silent darkness outside, gripped in suspense, waiting to see what happens next. Having witnessed the first act, the murder scene, only the finale remains.

He ordered me to stop, go clean. He would not have said that if I had money to give him. Why stop, when there is no pleasure in life without speed, no peace but in drugs. Send me mad will it? Kill ME will it? Well, HE is dead, not me. I live! HE is lifeless!

I am now but a silent judge of death, with all the long pointing fingers of shadows – the jury – around me. I could laugh. If I did I could break the spell gripping me – this infernal accusing silence. Why do I stay? I dare not answer. I do not really know the answer. I begin to fear.

A clock strikes the quarter hour – quarter to midnight. Still I cannot move. The mood changes, stark realisation is upon me. My feelings rebel. His face mocks me! I feel pity and horror for him. I was rash. God, why did I mix them? If ever I need a fix it's now. Why is the silence so accusing? Why does it hang so heavily about me? It descends like a leaden blanket upon me, shutting me in with my victim, smothering me.

He leers gloatingly up at me. Does he judge me now in death? Read me? Read my soul? I must get out of here, out of this coffin, out of death and into life, find people, find sound, find oblivion. My body aches. My legs feel unsteady. IT grins at me now and waits. It's coming closer. I mustn't fall. I'll be okay after I find where he hides his stash. I silently scream for that fix.

I'm tired. I'll lay down here for a while, and then I'll look around and find where he hides them.

The booming of a clock striking midnight cuts the air! A full moon rises above the window ledge. Its cold non-judgmental light floods the room. One body lies upon the other. They form a cross. One wears a frown and the other what appears to be a smile.

FOOTSTEPS IN THE NIGHT

THE OLD RUSTED UTILITY TRUCK came screeching to a stop outside the small town hotel where most of his fellow meat-workers called in on their way home from work. Nervous and excited, Bill quickly jumped out and slammed the door behind him.

He glanced anxiously around, ready for any possible confrontation with the unexpected. Seeing nothing unusual, he hurried to stand framed in the open doorway. In a high state of agitation he sucked hard on the thin 'roll-ya-own' cigarette he had squeezed almost flat between his broad thumb and first finger, before flicking it on to the stone floor. Without a downward glance he squashed the last spark of life out of it with his boot, while his gaze scanned the room, anxiously searching for his friend Doug.

As he edged further forward he spied Doug, whose large frame was propped up against the bar counter; his protruding stomach neatly tucked beneath its over-hang. As if he knew instinctively that his missing workmate had suddenly returned, Doug turned his sagging jowls to face the door. Without the slightest change of expression he acknowledged Bill's presence by nodding twice before turning back to the barmaid. "Pull me two beers this time Elsie," he ordered, idly noting Elsie's full breasts as they danced unconstrained beneath her thin cotton blouse. Unperturbed, she placed the wet glasses on the strip of towelling mat. Doug slowly picked them up in his callused hands and headed towards a vacant table.

Bill followed and without a word he slid his lean body into one of the plastic chairs. With a shaking hand he shoved his stained wide brimmed hat on the floor beneath. Blinking nervously he stared thirstily as Doug placed one of the beers in front of him. His hand shot out to grasp the glass, downing its contents in gulps.

"What's the hurry, mate?" enquired Doug as he squeezed himself into the seat opposite. "Take it slow."

"Strewth, ya don't know what a lifesaver it is to get a nice cold beer into ya. Life's been hell lately." He put down the empty glass and wiped his mouth with the back of his hand.

"Ain't seen you in weeks. What you been up to?"

"Ya just don't know the half of it. We had to move from that rented house we was in. Since then I ain't been able to go to work. Money's as scarce as hen's teeth and me missus won't let me out of 'er sight even though I keep tellin' her I've got to get back to work. This arvo I had to sneak out while she was hangin' out the washin'."

"You shifted? I thought you liked that old place although it was a bit out of town and a bit rundown but you said the rent was real cheap. I laughed when you told me your wife had a 'mickey' when she found a set of false teeth down the broken kitchen sink plug-hole on the day you moved in."

"Yeah, but the penny finally dropped. We found we had a non-paying guest we didn't know about."

"A guest? I'll make a guess. A kangaroo or an emu moved in with you." Doug laughed, and those seated nearby began to take an interest.

"Very funny, but you're right off the mark. What I'm gonna tell ya's true I swear. Ya can ask me missus if ya don't think I'm bein' fair dinkum."

"Okay, then it must have been a possum." Doug's grin was wide.

Bill ignored him. "Me missus got so scared she just about has me on a lead. Buy me a coldie Doug and I'll tell ya all about it."

"Okay, but it'd better be worth it. If you're waffling on to get free beer out of me you'll have to come up with a ripper of a yarn," said Doug as he headed for the bar.

As Bill mentally recalled the past month's happenings his pale drawn cheeks were beginning to flush. His eyes were wide and round and his hands began to shake once more.

A sudden scraping of chairs on the wooden floor behind Bill made him glance nervously around. The men at the next table had moved their chairs closer. Bill relaxed and smiled a slow smile. He knew that mentioning his mystery guest caused their interest.

Doug returned with fresh drinks. "I told Elsie what you said, and she's coming over to hear this fancy story of yours." He put the glasses down. Bill's hand gripped the closest. He quickly drained his." We did have an uninvited caller," insisted Bill.

"I still think you're having me on." Doug smirked.

"No, I ain't. Me son Tony'll back me up. Shout me another beer and I'll tell ya all about it. That last one didn't even touch the sides."

"Okay... you're on, but you owe me if this is a con job." Doug turned to Elsie who was gathering used glasses from a nearby table. "Elsie, another round." Elsie hastily retreated, to hurry back with the order.

"Ta," was Doug's response as he paid her. Being in no hurry to pass out of earshot, Elsie occupied herself by slowly wiping down the adjoining tables.

Bill, loving an audience, raised his voice for the benefit of the eavesdroppers. "It was in that old run-down homestead with the verandah all 'round that we rented just outside town. You know Doug." Doug nodded. "Everything was ridgy didge for a while. Then it started – every night when me and the missus'd got to bed – me trying to sleep but I can't 'cause the missus'd be shakin' me like blazes. Went crazy she did, every time the floorboards, especially the ones in the hall, creaked like someone was walkin' around the house.

I'd be swearin' at Maisie to shut up and go back to sleep 'cos I had to get up at the crack of dawn for work. But, do you think she'd listen…no… she'd grab me or thump me 'cause I wouldn't go and risk me neck. 'What if I'm right and it is a burglar?' she'd say

'Nothin' worth takin,' I'd say. Then she'd reckon it might be an escaped murderer or some criminal who'd been hidin' in the bush from the coppers, who'd attack us in our sleep. I told her it was a stray cat or possum that must've got in through the gap near the roof over the wood stove, and to shut up, but ya can't shut Maisie up when she's on a roll, but I begun to wonder about it a bit meself."

"All old houses creak like that. The floorboards shrink with age," said Doug, dripping sarcasm.

"Yeah, that's what I was tellin' Maisie. I kept harpin' at 'er but I may as well been talkin' to the flamin' wall. She was spooked." Bill paused, transferring his concentration to satisfying his almost endless thirst.

"Go on, get on with it. What happened next?" implored a now impatient Doug.

"Well the spooky stuff got worse." Bill began slowly. "One night when I'd a couple of mates over and we was havin' a drink or two in the kitchen, and talkin' about our 'visitor' and laughin' about it, when out of the blue the back door opened all by itself – no knock or nothin'. Then it closed again all by itself. Then it did it again. Blow me down… you wouldn't believe it if ya hadn't been there."

"Wind…that's what it was ... seen it in my own place. Doors suddenly slam shut ... wind," interjected Doug.

"I swear there was no wind. Take me word for it, 'cos it did it all over again. If there 'ad been wind, it wouldn't 'ave opened again. It'd 'ave stayed shut."

"Struth!" "Cricky!" Words of astonishment from those close by circled like an invisible halo in the air above Bill.

Doug scoffed. "Of course there was a wind. You and your mates were probably drunk as skunks and wouldn't have known Arthur from Martha."

Elsie, fearful a customer would draw her away before Bill finished, added, "Hurry up Bill or we'll be here all night."

Bill turned towards her. "Well there wasn't any wind," he said forcefully.

"Is that all? Are you finished? Is that your story?" queried Doug not concealing the disgust in his voice.

"I ain't finished. Get a load of this. 'Bout a week or so later on one of them real dark, no moon nights – no breeze or nothin'. me eighteen year-old – ya know Tony – was out with his mate. Around midnight I was dead asleep, but me missus woke me up talkin' loud in me ear as usual. 'There's Tony. I can hear those boots of his. I want you to tell him not to walk so heavy along the veranda. It wakes me up.'

Then we heard more footsteps comin' and we thought he'd brung his mate Johnny home. Johnny doesn't like to drive when he's 'ad too much grog 'cos he needs his licence for work. Then we heard a plonk when Tony tossed his gear inside his bedroom. Then he was out the door and on the verandah that runs almost round to the back of the house. Then we heard the two sets of footsteps following each other and keeping on going down the back stairs to the outside dunny. Then just as I'm trying to get back to sleep Maisie starts poking me in the ribs. 'It's Tony. He's calling you.' Maisie has good ears.

I listened real careful and she was right. It was Tony shoutin' 'Dad!' He sounded funny, scared like. I thought he must've made contact with that snake that hides behind the dunny seat, so I springs out of bed in the pitch black, feels me way to the back door and grabs the shovel I keep near the back steps just in case I ever needs it.

I stopped dead when I reached Tony. He was standin' there all by hisself at the shut dunny door. I was cursin' I hadn't grabbed me torch 'cos there was only a bit of a moon that'd just come up.

'What's all the squawking about Tony? Whose in the dunny?'

'I don't know." I never seen him so scared.

'Did ya see any strangers about?' I asked, but Tony said he 'aint.

I looked 'round for his mate. I thought, if it's not Maisie's night visitor it must be Tony's mate, maybe dead inside the dunny. 'That bloody snake musta got Johnny,' I said.

Bill stopped talking and gazed sadly at his empty glass. He muttered reproachfully, "Dry work talkin' like this all night."

"Another beer Elsie."

"You're a good mate Doug."

"Not if this turns out to be a dud of a story. Well, was Johnny dead?"

"I'm comin' to that, don't rush me. So I asks Tony. 'Johnny in there?'

'Nah,' he said, 'ain't Johnny.'

'Well tell me who it is,' I said to him. 'I know there was two of ya. Me and ya mum heard two lots of footsteps. Not some sheila is it? If it's a sheila you're a gonna.'

Then Tony put on that firm voice like he's speakin' to a kid. 'Dad, there's no one in there. When I came home there was someone walking ahead of me along the verandah. I thought it was you heading for the dunny. I wanted to go too, so I made off after you. When I got here there was no light coming through the cracks so I couldn't make out why you had the door shut. Thinking you might have croaked it or something I called 'Dad' a few times. When I didn't hear anything I pushed the door open and guess what, the dunny's empty. Have a look for yourself dad.'

"I did. I raised me shovel and pushed open the door that had swung shut and looked in. The dunny **was** empty!"

There was silence in the room as the implications of such a predicament registered in the surrounding brain cells. "I'm right, nothing but wind," Doug announced.

"No-one could make up a story like that, especially Bill," someone mouthed. "What happened then?"

"Well, Maisie cracked up when she found out. She claimed it must be the prowler she hears walking through the house at night. She nearly had a nervous breakdown I reckon. Did I have a time of it! I couldn't go to work. She claimed that the first thing a sex-maniac would do is dot the opposition on the head then have his evil way, so she didn't trust me to protect her, and I can tell ya fending her from a rapist was the last thing I wanted to do. So Maisie stayed awake every night expecting to be raped. She wore so much to bed a rapist wouldn't have had a chance unless he had all day to spare. One rainy night she wore her raincoat to bed in case she had to run for it.

She said she wanted us to leave. She said she didn't feel safe gettin' dressed or havin' a bath with eyes watching – feasting on her body. She never put up curtains – said we don't need 'em in the bush. I told her she wouldn't be so lucky, but that didn't come across too good. She said she'd die of fright if she saw him and I believe her. There was nothing else for it but to move.

I got on to the landlord and told him we was movin' 'cos

Maisie thought someone came into the house at night and she was scared. He laughed, really he did, and said, quite casual like, 'Perhaps it's a previous tenant. Some say they've seen him in the house, or walking around the place.' I tell him he wasn't makin' sense. 'If you know the bloke who's sneakin' round scarin' the day-lights out of people why don't ya do somethin' about it?' I asked, but the stupid man keep laughin' his head off. When he got his breath back he said, 'because I can't. He's a ghost.'

'Ghost? There ain't no ghosts.' I had to say that, even if it was giving me the jitters just thinking about it, 'course Maisie was listenin'. I told her to go and make a cup of tea but she wouldn't. 'What's 'is name? He's got to have a name.'

'Robert...' said the landlord. 'I forget his other name. He's supposed to haunt the place since he was found dead on the kitchen floor under VERY sus-picious circumstances as they say. He'd choked to death. His wife tried to revive him, but he'd conked out for good.'

"Well, whata ya know," commented Doug.

"Next thing, we're packin' and I'm lookin' for another house. Our landlord was a bit put out when I told him to get the last week's rent from the ghost; after all he's living there. Do ya know what me missus reckons happened to this Robert bloke?"

"No, what?"

"She says those false teeth we found clogging up the kitchen sink down-pipe must have been that Robert's. They must have fallen through the broken grid in the plughole. When the back door was opening that night it must have been him, comin' in to look for his teeth.' Then I got one of Maisie's 'if looks could kill' stares. She said, 'I bet I know why the poor coot choked to death. He was probably trying to eat some of that tough steak like you snitch from work. Same thing'll happen to us one day. You mark my words.'

There were a few sniggers of agreement from Bill's fellow meatworkers.

"Not a bad yarn but I still don't believe it was a ghost. The owner was probably having you on. Maybe he wanted you to go for some reason of his own. That's what I think. Anyway, where did you move to?"

"To old Charlie's place. He died remember, a few months back." Bill gazed meaningfully at his empty glass. "Another beer Doug?"

"Nah, not on your life. I'm getting home to tell Jean what happened to you and Maisie. She won't believe it either." He stood and stretched himself.

As he walked away, Elsie reluctantly headed to the bar to attend to several familiar new arrivals. "Go over and get Bill to tell you what he told Doug," she advised them. "A likely story, but it's a beautie. What do you want to drink...the usual?"

"Spot on Elsie old girl," was the reply as they sat down at Bill's table.

"What's your yarn Bill? Elsie seems to think it's worth hearing," one asked.

"I swear it's true. You can ask Maisie or me boy. I don't mind tellin' it again, but it's dry work talkin' all the time."

"Okay Elsie another beer...for Bill."

As Bill was about to begin his story for the second time, Elsie, with a tray of beer, hurried briskly back to Bill's side. She put them down.

"Sorry Bill, but Maisie just rang. She sounded very upset, and very angry. She said you're a creep for sneaking out and leaving her alone...reckons she saw the previous owner, dead Charlie, down in that far paddock chopping wood...says it must be him with that red hair and all. She's scared stiff and has locked herself in, and you'll have to shout out her middle name when you get to the door or she won't open it. Says you've got to come home this minute and do something...chase him away, she said."

"So he's still there choppin'?" Elsie nodded.

Bill was silent as his beer was being paid for and another ordered. He picked up his glass and half smiled. "I'll drink me beer first, don't want to offend me generous mates, and I've got a story to tell. Maisie and Charlie can wait. There's a lot of wood. He can keep chopping. Cheers!"

CRY OF THE WIND

THE CIVIL WAR IN IRELAND had continued on for so long and caused so much bloodshed and misery. Yet it had produced those who wanted peace so deeply they believed in their heart that it was attainable. They hated no one. They would save a life, any life, if they could…regardless.

•••••••••••••••••

"They know." Patrick's mother said. "They know it was you who helped smuggle O'Malley, our wounded leader, across to that English hospital, just as they were about to capture him. Go away somewhere safe. They know. Stacey warned us. So be very careful and don't try bringing any more wounded home. You can't save everyone."

"I must try," was his answer. As he left, he called back when he reached the gate. "Mother, I'll be home for tea."

•••••••••••••••••

I don't know how much time has passed since I felt all sight vanish as I collapsed. It was close to sunset, but I'm conscious now. My body feels numb and the blood has congealed on my chest and face. I know shock will keep me, for at least a while, from feeling pain from the bullet that struck me down. It happened while I was dragging a wounded friend to the shelter of trees. I felt a shooting pain as a bullet grazed my head. A second entered my back and the pain was sudden and fierce. Anthony now lies close by, not breathing.

The attack was brutal. My coat has gone, my trousers torn. As the temperature begins to drop I lay still, frightened to move. I want to drift off but grass seeds brush across my face, as the tall weeds are fanned by a fresh breeze; a breeze that is unfettered, loose, has no conflicting restrictions, while we live, controlled and motivated by the very conventions and prejudices we fight against. We struggle for freedom and lawful unrestricted movement but it keeps eluding us. I sigh and feel envious.

Time ticks by. No one comes by. There is no sound of traffic, or bikes, or feet, or human activity close by. A wild bird calls. What bird? Have you a name? Everything has a name. A name can bring forth love, but also hate, as I well know.

Rising out of the fading day come village sounds like waves warm and gentle. Mother will have lit the open fireplace by now – waiting – waiting for me.

My world and my life in it, passes before me. I grimace. In some future history book I will be but a name, forming part of the total number of those whom God has chosen for his cause for freedom in Ireland.

I think of those millions outside our struggle. Are they alive, or merely phantoms? Is this country alone, with a world of people around, circling us, never still, never touching? Do they understand our plight? Perhaps, but not to the extent I would like.

There is a complete aloneness in suffering, in dying. Why was it my fate to care when so many others don't? God alone knows, but does he care? I believe he does but is he listening?

My legs and feet are cold. Where are my shoes? They took my shoes and my jacket. My arms are beginning to freeze. The world itself is cold in many ways. I feel waves of despair and hatred lapping at my brain. I cannot let it drown me.

I see lights flicker and dance in the air between my village and the next town. A familiar picture takes shape in my mind, of army trucks with glaring lights that blind the eyes. I hear the sound of metal, guns, followed by flesh in pain or shouts of joyous victory – all familiar. The smudge of yellow-gold brightness I now see in the sky over the town is of a fire somewhere.

'Don't be late home son. I'll be worried. They know.' I hear my mother say.

"I'm coming mother."

I struggle, but at last I rise. Pain shoots through my body as I stand upright. I scream out. I feel the trickling of blood on my face. I wipe my eyes. I walk slowly in the semi-darkness with my hand stretched out in front of me. My mother is waiting with my dinner. "Yes mother, I'm on my way home so don't worry," I mutter.

I slide to the wet ground – hard and pitiless, and the blackness outside joins the dark inside and for a while I neither feel nor think.

I become aware of someone in front of me. *Mother?* I open my eyes wide. Somehow with little effort I rise to my feet. I stare at the figures before me, fascinated. They move towards me. Suddenly I am clasped in the arms of my brother, while my uncle watching, smiles at me. Both lost lives in the battle for freedom. A feeling of utter contentment settles over me. My part in the struggle is over. The physical shell has played out its part. My spirit is joining other souls to form a gigantic wave of inspiration for peace, for those still alive. Eventually this peace will show up in all their lives. I now know that nothing I have done has been in vain.

"Mother do not cry. "

....

It was mid-morning when the British Army jeep stopped. A sergeant and a private jumped out. The private looked at the two crumpled untidy heaps in the long grass at the side of the path and said with astonishment.

"Why, this one's smiling Sergeant, like he's asleep and dreaming."

"Yes," answered the Sergeant thoughtfully as he turned back to the jeep to call for a stretcher, "and sometimes dreams come true."

CHEEKY CHARLIE MEETS HIS MATCH

CHARLIE WITHERS, HIS RUGGED SUN-BROWNED FACE scraped almost pink from his recent close shave, was dressed in his safari jacket, well-worn 'best' shirt, and as a concession to Pearl, he wore his black tight pointed-toed shoes. He sat stiffly in the darkened theatre, his gnarled fingers nervously twisting the programme while juggling a large packet of popcorn on his knees. Patience was not a virtue of Charlie's, but he intended to make this night one to remember, a milestone in his life – a change in fortune, so a rein on his impetuous nature had to be maintained.

Charlie was infatuated with Pearl Starr of THE HEAVENLY PEARL OF THE STARR CIRCUIT show. His bedroom walls were covered with her pictures, as was his work place at the abattoirs. When he bought a ticket to her concert he was convinced that his number would be drawn out at the theatre where supper with Pearl after the show was the prize.

He had announced to his workmates, 'I know I'll win.' He had waved the ticket in front of them. It was number 96. 'Sure thing. It's what they call fate. Pearl and I'll end up together. I know it every time I look at her photo. It's her and me. What a pair we'll make.

After tonight I won't be working here anymore. It's a cert I can get her to make me her manager. After all I worked once for an accountant and I know 'the ropes.' Nothing to figures – you just copy down what other people tell you or give you on bits of paper.

'Why'd you leave that cushy job if you know so much?' another had asked.

'All boiled down to jealousy. I told the boss I could do a better job than him and asked for a raise, and he sacks me.'

'Bit of a come-down workin' here, ain't it?' sneered his offsider.

'Only temporary; only temporary.'

Charlie had patted his workmate on the back then hurried away. His thoughts were on what a lot he had to do – go home, get dressed and be at the theatre well before the curtain rose.

His thoughts as he reclined in the soft theatre seat, reverted back to Pearl. Meeting her personally would be his dream come true. It would be his big chance. He could picture them together and his flight of fancy took on a life of its own. He pictured the scene as he stuffed popcorn into his mouth. *Me and Pearl will be alone together after the show. There will be candlelight. There always is...seen it many times at the flicks. Then she'll melt in my arms, like when I have my way with Violet down at the pub when I pat her knee or squeeze her buttocks.*

He planned to gaze into Pearl's eyes and say, 'I love you. Now we've found each other we could be together all the time if you give your Charlie a job.' He could imagine her replying. 'Of course, Charlie – I like that name Charlie. Now we've met, your wish is my command.'

His whole body thrilled at the thought. After all he knew he was good looking in a rugged sort of way although somewhat overweight, but a few beers less a night would soon fix that, but he decided she would probably prefer him the way he was. He did not have any trouble getting admiring looks and easy dates down at the local, 'The Sailor's Anchor.'

Charlie recalled when he had once worked in a theatre as a cleaner and watched the shows, and it seemed to Charlie that managers only checked bookings, and came to watch and look important during rehearsals. He felt he knew the 'ropes' there too. *I'll tell her I'll give my services free first off and accept any job, but paperwork would suit me best. Then I'll take control of her accounts and in no time I'll be her manager. It'll be a pushover. Once Pearl realises she can't do without me, which shouldn't take long, I'll propose –* **Mr** *Pearl Starr.* He savoured the mental image of a wedding she would be happy to pay for. But Charlie was not silly. *There must be other men in her life, but once I become her manager I'll . . .*

He briefly held his breath as the lights in the plush theatre faded slowly casting the theatre into darkness. A sudden bright light focused on the stage as the horizontal centres of the red velvet curtain were being tugged upwards by invisible cords, and the orchestra began playing, in readiness for Pearl to perform her famous dance and singing act.

The curtain rose and the great Pearl Starr herself appeared to float on to the stage. The crowd roared and got to their feet, Charlie with them. A mass of blonde curls framed her delicately made-up face and cascaded around her shoulders and halfway down her taut back. Her red pouting lips fascinated her male fans. She would hold the gaze of any fan lucky enough to have her look directly at them for a few seconds. Long enough to send a thrill that put their nerves into delicious turmoil. To Charlie no words could describe her sexiness.

As she stopped centre stage the audience slowly re-seated themselves and the production unfolded, full of glittering professionalism. As she sang she glided from one side of the stage to the other like a skater on ice. Her low-cut green velvet dress with its sequins gleaming and winking at the audience hugged her well-proportioned body. A long shapely leg ending in a high-heeled glitter-sprinkled white velvet shoe appeared briefly from a slit in her tight skirt, promising more to come.

Charlie mentally caressed her body as his gaze travelled upwards from ankle to her almost completely exposed breasts. He wondered why he had never met a woman who had shapely breasts like Pearl's, with their unblemished pink smoothness. Charlie's excitement grew as he pictured his hand gripping them in the height of passion.

The soft deep husky voice of the singer denoted desire and promise as she sang the words, which to Charlie, were meant only for him. 'I want **you**, lover boy... lover boy... don't be coy, lover boy." Charlie clutched the arms of the seat in the excitement of anticipation.

The finale was even more spectacular. Pearl the professional whipped her admirers into a frenzy of desire and admiration, as they were sucked into the magic of lights and sound combined. When she sang the last few lines she bowed her head slightly and sang secretly, huskily, as the curtain began to close slowly. The audience rose as one body and clapped, whistled and shouted – Charlie with them. Slowly impatience grew within him and he wished they would all shut up so as he could get his time with

Pearl.

Finally the curtain re-opened and the manager came from the wings to join Pearl on stage. He reminded everyone the winner would come up on to the stage, meet the star and then join her for supper. Silence reigned as Pearl's long fingers with their pink lacquered nails made a delicate circle in the air, before reaching into the barrel to draw out a single ticket. Suspense turned electric throughout the hall. She handed the ticket to her manager. He read out the winning number. It was number 96.

Charlie was already on his feet and roughly pushed past those who unfortunately sat between him and the aisle, stamping on some toes as he squeezed past them. In his haste he failed to notice the attractive short-skirted usherette assigned to him, who, smiling, and with outstretched hand was to lead him down the aisle to the stage. He left her behind. She ran with a model-like swing of hips after him as he ran down the aisle and up the stairs and on to the stage, where Pearl was watching and waiting beside her manager.

On stage he ignored the welcoming manager who was ready to shake his hand and congratulate him. He felt an instant jealous reaction as he briefly glimpsed the smooth professional smile on the manager's face. *I'll fix him first thing. He's gone.*

He headed directly towards the smiling beauty with his large rough hand outstretched. He grabbed hers in his and she winced under his grip. She struggled to keep smiling and turned her face to the audience so those taking photos would capture her 'happiness'.

"Pleased to meet ya Pearl love. I'm Charlie," he announced as the dismayed usherette stood frozen below the stage.

The furious manager, bustling quickly after Charlie, knew he had failed in his attempt to introduce this uncouth winner to Pearl and make the small talk necessary to please the patrons.

Pearl pursed her full sensual lips. "Hello, lucky winner. Looking forward to supper are you?" she cooed – her voice coming from deep in her chest. She quickly switched off her microphone as she read the desire in his ogling eyes.

Move Over James Bond

"I'm looking forward to having more than supper with you," he whispered as his bushy eyebrows were raised. He followed with a 'wink wink, nudge nudge'. The crowd whistled as their imagination took over.

"Oh... an optimist are you?" Pearl spoke quietly. Charlie was not listening. Excitement at her nearness overwhelmed him and the words had no meaning.

He continued. "I know we're going to get along famously. I've waited for this for a long time...well... so now it's no time like the present time, or should I say no time like supper-time for discussing business with pleasure. Is it love? I have a proposition. You're going to love having me around...but first things first..."

The manager, recovering from his initial horror, quickly slapped on his stage smile. He moved forward and announced to the audience, who had become restless at not hearing what was being said. "Thank you ladies and gentlemen. There'll be another happy winner at our next show. Pearl loves you all." The clapping was deafening.

Pearl's expression had not changed even minutely except for the blue eyes darkening with contempt as she looked at this over-confident man. *'He must have kangaroos loose in his top paddock to think I'd be interested in* **him** *– another drab bore. The cheek of him wanting to be a permanent fixture. Why I let my manager talk me into this publicity stunt I don't know.*

She turned, still smiling broadly as she faced the clapping crowd. She stretched out her arms to embrace the audience and bowed her head towards them. Charlie did the same. The red velvet curtain dropped quickly.

As they walked off, Pearl now relaxes, chuckled to herself. *Thank God my manager will be joining us for supper. There's no mention of dining alone with the winner. I'll speak to him on the quiet beforehand about what I'm planning. He may object, but I'll love to see this cheeky Charlie's face when I take off my wig and he sees my short black hair, and, I get everyone around us to call me Percy, not Pearl. I can hardly wait.*

IN THE NICK OF TIME

SOME SAY ALL THINGS ARE ALREADY PLANNED – that we have no say in what happens to us, or how we turn out in this life. It's not our doing. But that was not what Ross Brown's family believed, although they failed to convert Ross no matter how they tried. He would not see the 'light'. He scoffed at any suggestion of an after-life and a God of any persuasion. He was the despair of those who loved him because they believed and he did not. Bone-lazy Ross, atheist and drunk, had hidden his 'vices' when he fell in love with a devout churchgoer Agnes, who on discovering Ross's flaws was on a 'mission.'

Ross's motto was, 'Drink and be merry for tomorrow we die, and avoid anything that resembles work.' But his wife Agnes never lost faith that he would 'turn around.' All her efforts failed until she had a brainwave. She began serving him dry breakfast cereal for his dinner. "What's this rubbish?" he demanded, pushing the plate away.

Agnes stood feet apart and glared down at him. "And that's what you'll be getting from now on until you get back on the straight and narrow. I want you to see the vicar. He'll help you. If you won't, then you can cook your own dinner from now on."

That was exactly what lazy Ross did not want. Up to that moment he had managed to avoid all kitchen duties. He could not remember ever boiling an egg. He decided what was the lesser of the two evils. "Of course I will my dear. You should have asked me before."

Agnes gave a loud "Huh!" and went to the phone to make an appointment with the vicar. Satisfied, she disappeared into the kitchen to make Ross some sausages and vegetables. *I can't let him go hungry.*

The vicar was well aware, through Agnes, of Ross's shortcomings and decided that this was the answer to both his and Agnes' prayers.

The visit was short and afterwards Ross, now in the pub, proudly told his drinking mates, "I converted the vicar, not the other way round. He agreed with me that I was a great bloke and nearly perfect, except for an occasional over indulgence in the good red stuff which you blokes force on me."

"How did you manage to do that? He's no pushover," asked one of his intrigued listeners.

"Easy...I told him we were drinking Bailey's non-alcoholic drink, and we were, but what he didn't know was that I'd laced it with gin. By the time he could get out his sermon he was slurring his words and agreeing with everything I said. Then he slid to the floor and fell asleep."

His drinking mates were jubilant. After clapping him on the back several times, they bought him several rounds of drinks to celebrate his brilliance.

Ross's liver eventually objected and he was prostrate with agony.

With much pushing and shoving and talking non-stop, Agnes got him to the hospital. The doctor preformed what was a serious operation and it was touch and go for Ross. Agnes, believing Ross would be lost in the next world as he was in this one so – as was her want – called in the vicar.

"As it is the will of God that you are about to depart from this world, just remember, God is waiting for you at the judgement table," expounded the vicar to the semi-conscious Ross. "Repent of your sins now and you will be rewarded with forgiveness."

Ross was not too far gone as yet and decided that maybe it would be a good idea if he did get on God's good side – if there was a God – ask for forgiveness just in case, although he could not think of anything he ever did that could be called a sin. But, he knew what both the vicar and his family wanted him to say. He'd make them happy now that death was closing in on him.

"I repent any bad habits I might have that I don't know about," he whispered. "From this moment on I give up the grog and all my other vices, not that I have any," and his eyes closed.

"Rest in peace now Ross," comforted the satisfied vicar although 'just in the nick of time' had been his first thought, while Agnes screamed for the doctor. He raced in armed with his stethoscope and followed by a nurse with a needle in her hand.

"Has Ross gone to his eternal rest?" the distraught Agnes whispered.

....

Meanwhile Ross had arrived at the pearly gates. He saw no one and was about to enter when up dashed St Peter. "Just a moment Ross. We have rules here...no drunks allowed in heaven, except of course for a few cardinals. You have to go back and show us you really have reformed before we can allow you in."

"Hold on, I'm on the wagon now," said Ross, and he began to walk towards the gates and into heaven, but St Peter was too quick. With one wave of his hand the door slammed shut. "Just in the nick of time," muttered St. Peter.

....

Back at Ross's bedside the doctor pounded Ross's chest and the family wrung their hands, cried, or both, until the vicar began to lead them in prayers. They prayed loudly so they could be heard 'up there'.

After minutes, which seemed to be an eternity to the family, his eyes slowly opened. He looked up at the smiling happy faces of his family and the satisfied expression on the face of the vicar.

"He's stable now and his chances of recovery are excellent," stated the doctor.

Ross listened. *Goodo, the boys at the pub'll be pleased.* He then remembered his vow.

"S-h-i-t!" he exclaimed soundlessly.

BEYOND THE BLACK STUMP

I LIE WITH MY FACE TO THE SKY, footsore, weary, without food, shelter; lost since I left my broken-down 'bomb' of a car somewhere out there on the road to Alice Springs.

The bare skin of my sun-burnt arms and legs feel the cool freshness of the long grass beneath this old gum tree, unconfined, wild, as is my mind, my thoughts, yet subdued and controlled by the rules prevailing in my own society.

I keep very still. Completely exhausted I can do nought else. I feel the first strong breath of wind from the east. It grapples with every living thing around me – plays with them until it tires, then rests, then plays again, making sport of all but me, though it tears at my hair; blinds me with its growing force against my pupils. I feel strangely envious of its freedom. It has no home like me, but unlike me, it can make itself at home anywhere. Like me it can be calm, be violent. I know it is happiest in the trees when I hear it laugh among the branches while their multiple leaves dance and whisper together.

This day, my day, goes by in fitful dozing, my body too exhausted to rise, to move on. I brush away an insect from my face, a petty thing to come intruding in my musings. The wind drops its force, retreats. I now relax as the day, designed, created, to circle the globe, travels on to another world unseen – a world I will never know.

Time ticks away. I watch the countryside become drenched in the colour of amber as the sun hovers over the horizon's rim, but it quickly changes, to be rainbowed in rose-pink hues. I feel woven somehow into being part of nature, as dusk begins to settle like a huge net over all, without sound, without hindrance.

My body, my nerves, all jerk as a kookaburra laughs, near, now far. Eerie silence envelops me. I'm alone again.

I force my mind back to the people I left behind – the ones I love – so few. Are they happy? Do they sometimes think of me? Others...so many... one forgets. I recall hate, fear, love. All touched me, but no longer deeply. I feel the air grow cold. It encases my shorts-clad legs, my arms, my body. Am I destined to lie here, for all eternity? One tear rises in each eye to trickle to the ground, unheeded, lonely, just two, so few.

The trees become blurred shapes, partners of shadows. The grass turns darker, colder, wet. I breathe in deep as I suck in dew, invigorating and satisfying to my soul in anguish.

A star is born. It winks at me – one star in a sky immense, deep blue, two stars, thousands. A smudge of light now rises from behind the distant horizon, like a candle shaded by a hand. Below a brow of orange, a shy moon begins to peep over. I wait. I watch it expand to complete roundness; it's calming light blanketing the earth. The trees no longer darkish blurs now separate their shapes once more, to stand out in the mellow light, not cold and taut as in the steamy day,

Thick grey clouds begin to stream up from that other hidden world. They spread out across the sky, grow in density, then separate into restless streaks – one star swallowed, two stars – more. Cotton clouds drift over the moon to snuff out its light... gone, extinguished. I am alone again.

I watch the moon dodge clouds, vanishing completely, to reappear again and again as the game goes on.

A shiver is felt in the leaves above, around. The wind, returns, strikes. The tree sighs. Is it echoing my despair? I can't stay! I raise my head. I take deep breaths. I stare outward, once more desperately scanning everything in view.

Suddenly I rub my eyes as a nomad would on spying an oasis in the desert. Is it real, that fingertip of light, winking, beckoning, dancing between a crowd of trees at the bottom of the rise? I am renewed of hope, but am I hallucinating...dreaming? Is that a house among the trees? Hope grows.

I force myself to scramble unsteadily to my feet. My body aches, my limbs are weak, but I must try. I lean against the tree. I fill my lungs with the cold air as a renewed wind spits, stings me with dust and sand-like specks. I steady myself against the tree trunk. Its roots, like my feet, stay firm. It's leaves, like my hair, are slaves to it. A bond springs up between nature and me. I feel it – endearing, binding.

I hoist up my backpack, long since empty of any sustenance

and begin the downward trek. I'm sliding now, almost slipping on loose dirt. A branch I grab like a hand outstretched. It keeps me upright...a friend...no, just a tree, wild, easily forgotten.

Regaining my balance I stumble on my clumsy feet, sore, blistered, downwards, towards the beckoning light. I hit level ground and my boots scrape on gravel.

I'm on a road, white and winding in the moonlight. It has been waiting for me all the time. With exhilaration I keep going...at times almost overcome by the desire to sink to the ground and not move...perhaps ever.

Time seems to stretch out to infinity, but the light ahead keeps luring me on and on, closer, closer.

I hear a raised voice. A light blinds me from an open door. I crumble. Arms and warmth embrace me. I'm safe.

YESTERDAY'S SANTA

EDNA STARED IN AMAZEMENT at her seventy-five-year-old husband, Stan.

"That's Colin's Santa costume you've got on, isn't it? I recognise that odd button he sewed on when he couldn't find the one he lost."

Stan slowly turned completely around, expecting Edna to admire him in the role of Santa. Instead she was frowning. He pouted. "Yes, it's Colin's. He asked me to take his place at the supermarket 'cos his kid's sick. 'Why not?' I said. 'I've got the shape for it.' He patted his red, jacket-covered rotund body then stroked his white beard. "My face is perfect too".

His wife shook her head in disbelief.

Annoyed at her lack of approval Stan demanded. "Well! Why not?"

"I'll tell you why not. You're too old for one thing. And you haven't got the patience, especially with the kids in this neighbourhood. Never been raised with any respect for anyone. More petty crime here than in the rest of the city."

"You're exaggerating. Kids are just kids, naughty sometimes, but innocent little mites. I'm going to love it."

"Changed your tune now have you? You hated them last week." In all their fifty years of marriage, Edna had never won an argument with Stan. He believed that his views, opinions, and decisions were never wrong, so it was fruitless to argue with him, but this time she felt he needed some advice. "Maybe you'll enjoy it but the kids won't. You're too out-spoken, so think before you speak or you could be in trouble."

Peeved by her criticism Stan insisted. "I just like to let people know when they're in the wrong and set them on the right track. Nothing wrong with that."

"Well, you'd better watch your temper or you'll have some angry parent coming down hard on you."

"Don't worry. I've handled worst than a few cheeky kids in my time." He ambled towards the front door.

Edna shrugged as she walked to the kitchen. She knew he

would be ready for a strong cup of tea and several hot scones when he returned. As she baked she tried to picture some customer trying Stan's patience and chuckled.

Her cooking finished, Edna decided she would go and see how Stan was getting on. 'It should prove very interesting,' she thought.

At the store Edna kept out of range of Stan's vision and watched.

The Christmas spirit was very much alive. Stan was seated amidst the decorated Christmas trees and plaster reindeers, hemmed in by the bustle of people purchasing gifts, while the background sound of Christmas carols stirred happy memories for all.

Stan felt very pleased with himself. The morning had passed without incident. He had happily promised children whatever gifts they asked for. With self-control he did not know he possessed, he refrained from telling them not to press their discarded gum on to his collar and to keep their sticky fingers off his beard. He had also successfully held his temper when some mothers plonked their infants, wet-bottomed from leaking nappies, on his knee. He now felt he was perfect for the job and Colin could stay away as long as he wanted to.

Suddenly a large woman, a larger man, and an ungainly boy confronted him. The woman was outfitted in tight two-way stretch pants and top, both at least two sizes too small for her plump figure. Stan felt he should tell her to go to 'Vinnies' or the 'Salvos' for something that fitted, but held his tongue.

Her companion was a down-at-thong-heel, unwashed, loose-fat-carrying, pie-eating male. Gravy dribbled down his chin. Stan shuddered and looked at the boy. He was a grubby-faced American-street-kid clone in clothes to fit an adult. His cap was on back-to-front and he was blowing out a mouthful of stretched bubble gum that snapped back on to his dirty face. He clutched a paper cup full of juice in one grimy hand.

Stan was not unduly concerned. The boy looked about ten. At that age, they rejected any invitation to converse with Santa. However, this one, to Stan's surprise walked over, obviously wanting to sit on his knee. Getting close, the boy purposely stamped on Stan's arthritic big toe. Stan gritted his teeth to control himself, holding his breath for a few seconds to prevent a verbal onslaught directed towards the boy, now seated firmly on his knee. He tried to ignore the hot peppermint bubble gum breath assaulting his face. Suddenly the boy's free hand gripped a handful of Stan's beard. He pulled hard, almost ripping it out by the roots. "That's cool! It's real, Mum," he shouted.

Stars circled Stan's vision. The desire to backhand the boy had risen instantaneously but instead he pushed the boy roughly off his knee. Once upright the boy turned his cup of sticky juice upside down. Stan jumped to his feet as juice trickled down his pants to form a sticky puddle on the floor. The woman shrieked with glee. The male grinned widely. The child smirked. Stan's face glowed with rage.

"What kind of a useless individual are you raising?" he loudly demanded.

The woman's voice dripped with sarcasm. "Santa's gonna cry 'cos Santa's upset at a little boy who accidentally spilt his drink."

"I reckon he should buy Reggie another drink," leered the man.

Stan stepped closer to the couple, no longer conscious of anything but the taunting pair. "Take my word for it," he shouted. "That kid of yours is fodder for the crime machine. Take my advice and get him back on the right track! Give him some discipline before he becomes an adult monster."

"How dare you call our little boy a monster." She raised her voice, while her lips remained in a smirk. "The only monster is you. You big fat fake."

Stan was wound up. Nothing, not even Edna, could stop him now. "Wake up to yourself before it's too late – although looking at you both it's probably too late already."

"Now this will STOP. IMMEDIATELY!"

Stan recognised the voice of the manager who had forced his way between the gathering bystanders. He gripped Stan's arm in an effort to pull him away. Stan did not budge, but struggled to regain his inner composure. The manager being unsuccessful, squeezed himself between Stan and the irate couple. His smile was sickly sweet as he spoke. "Madam, sir, I'm sure this can be settled amicably."

Stan's stomach turned over. He was speechless for once.

"You're... so... kind." The mother had suddenly acquired a catch in her voice. "This man." She began jabbing her finger in Stan's direction, "insulted us, and treated our dear Reggie real bad. I think it's called abuse or assault, isn't it Dougie?"

"Sure is." Dougie raised his eyebrows at Stan. "People can be sued for that."

"Perhaps you'd like to come to my office to discuss it? What a nice lad you have. Perhaps we can find a gift for him. We pride ourselves on making our customers happy. This way please." The manager began to move away. As he passed Stan, he said quietly from the corner of his mouth, "Get your things, you're fired."

The boy's father snarled as he brushed past Stan. "In future don't mess with your superiors – bum face!"

The boy followed, walking slowly. He made a huge bubble with his gum. It burst over his nose and chin. "Want some?" was his cheeky offer.

Stan was livid. He now felt he could not get out of the drink-sodden Santa outfit and the store quick enough. Unhappily he pictured Edna saying, 'I told you, didn't I?'

On his arrival home Edna watched the despondent man as he entered the hall. She had never before seen such a hangdog expression on his face.

"I got fired," Stan mumbled sheepishly. Then trying to regain some of his lost pride he added forcefully, "It was a set-up, Edna. I should have seen it coming." He fell silent, and Edna waited. When he spoke again his speech was slow and thoughtful, almost humble, unlike the Stan Edna knew so well.

"You were right, Edna. I'm too old and too impatient for such a caper. The world of Santa Claus I understand belongs to yesterday."

She decided not to tell him she had witnessed the whole disastrous scene. She wanted to say, 'Serve you right, you silly old man. I warned you but you never learn,' but then, it occurred to her that perhaps he had learnt something. After all the years of believing himself to be infallible, he had admitted for the first time that she was right and he was wrong. Edna smiled quietly with a lift of her heart, convinced it was *one of those Christmas miracles you hear about.*

She took hold of her husband's hand and in genuine sympathy gently said, "Come dear, I think you need something stronger than tea. I'll pour you a beer." She led the sad, disappointed man into the kitchen.

As she handed him his filled beer mug he looked up into her face and smiled in sudden appreciation and contentment. "How do you put up with an old codger like me?"

Edna, clever as she was did not answer. She smiled and thought, 'When next the silly old man comes up with any more of his stupid ideas I'll remind him of how this turned out. Perhaps even on other occasions as well.'

She said. "Have another scone, Dear."

YOUR MOTHER HAS TO GO

ALEX, ABOUT TO LEAVE FOR WORK, raised his voice as he farewelled his wife at the open front door. His gold-embossed leather briefcase was gripped fiercely in one hand.

"I'm sorry Helen, but I'm very tired of your mother living with us. It's been ten months now, and I've had enough! She's got to go!"

Realising her husband's normally tightly controlled anger was about to explode, Helen half-closed the door. No need to involve the neighbours. "Alex... please.... Not so loud. Mother might hear you."

"SHE won't. SHE wouldn't be up yet!" he remarked sarcastically.

Helen sighed, resigned to hear what she had expected to hear months ago as Alex struggled with impatience at her mother's actions. She scanned her husband's face anxiously as he continued. "It's just as well she DOES sleep in! I'd hate to listen to her whingeing first thing in the morning. If she's not moaning that her arthritis hurts, it's the dog barking, or the cat gives her an allergy, or the lounge is too lumpy. On top of all that, the kids are always squabbling because they have to share the same bedroom. Last night was the last straw when she wandered into our bedroom without even knocking. We have no privacy. She's killing our marriage. "

"She can't help it. She's not well."

"Well, I've had ENOUGH! She's always criticising, always wants something different from what we're eating at mealtime. She's always demanding something, like a glass of water to take her pills AFTER we've gone to bed. She has you running after her all the time."

"Alex, you know mother has nowhere else to go except here with her own family." Her tone was pleading, although she realised how trying her mother could be.

"With all the complaints she claims she has, why not a nursing home? That's where she should be. AND she'd be well looked after."

"You may be right, but she is still my mother, and I wouldn't like her to be in a place she hated... But...." Desperate to put this disagreement behind her, Helen recalled past conversations with her mother. "There IS one place she seems to like. She's mentioned it a few times... Crescent Waters, a retirement village... but it's costly. She can't afford it."

"Well, I've given it a lot of thought. I don't care WHAT it costs to get her out, and KEEP her out, just do it. To hell with the expense! Your mother must go!"

Helen's eyes widened in amazement. Although Alex's bank accounts were bulging, he parted with money only when forced to. "Oh Alex, I never realised how much she has upset you." In an effort to calm him, and hide her growing excitement at his offer she whispered, "Thank you darling."

"If it gets her out of our hair I'll consider the money well spent."

Helen stepped back. "Don't be late for work dear. I'll ring Crescent Waters straight away. I hope I can persuade mother to go there."

"Good luck. You'll need it." Alex gave her a quick wave as he climbed into the car and drove away.

Helen frowned with worry as she closed the door. What if her mother refused to go? Life would become unbearable with Alex feeling the way he did. Footsteps made her turn quickly. Startled, she saw her mother walking towards her. Guilt washed over her.

"I heard it all dear." There was a catch in her mother's voice, causing Helen to experience a sinking feeling in the pit of her stomach. "I know he doesn't want me here, and I'm an extra burden for you. So, for your sake, I'd go into that place... Crescent Waters. But, unfortunately, I haven't that sort of money."

Helen was relieved it was her mother and not she who first brought up the subject. The feeling of guilt lifted. "Then you must have heard Alex say he'd pay for everything. I'll ring them later. Now, don't worry. I'll arrange everything."

Soon after Helen had left to finalise arrangements, her mother hurried to the telephone. She dialled Unit 5, Crescent Waters. When the receiver was picked up at the other end her voice screeched with excitement.

"That you George? It's Millie. I've got great news dear. Helen's rich skinflint of a husband's finally coming up with the money. It's taken me a lot of effort to get Alex so fed up he's agreed to finance my move to Crescent Waters. I feel sorry for what I've put Helen through, but I had to do something, and I'll make it up to her later . . .

What's that George? . . . Yes I AM clever. The long wait is almost over, and no-one's going to separate us again, Darl. Perhaps we should have shocked everyone by admitting we were... err... close, before our units were sold from under us and you went to Crescent Waters. But isn't it wonderful? We'll be close again...

What are you saying George? I can't understand you... Oh George! Don't get so emotional. Stop sniffling old man or I'll start. Think of the good times ahead of us. See you soon. Bye... I've got to start packing!"

MARCIA'S TRIP TO MARS: YEAR 2055

Dear Diary.
MARS HAS NOT BEEN FULLY COLONISED YET – much of it is still unexplored – but I'm in one of the initial groups due to my ex-husband being a city father. This is his way of getting out of supporting me under the divorce settlement, the weasel. I could have refused but it might be fun, and so I chose to escape the smouldering earth, now almost devoid in parts of most items of sustenance.

On this first rocket ship we'll be packed like sardines, so we can take only bare necessities. No more than a backpack, I was informed. I'll make MINE a big one. First they said, 'Take what we like'. That was before that second nitrogen, nuclear, or whatever, bomb, set off a chain reaction circling the earth, exploding bombs other countries had ready to use if necessary.

Some of us from yet unaffected parts have to get out before it spreads to us or so they say, but people do get carried away at times.

The problem is what to take? Some of us accustomed to every whim and desire being fulfilled on this once plentiful earth, have to make very difficult choices. How much money, gold, jewellery will I need to exchange, to bribe? Will it be of value also to any natives living there? The authorities say 'There are none,' but they are not sure really, and there'll be our own mob of grabbers and shysters ready to fleece you.

Water – limited they say, but sufficient – enough for a spa bath in my own private quarters I imagine.

Food could be a problem. Will there be enough? They have only basic stuff there I believe. How can I do without unsalted, polyunsaturated butter, my favourite low-cal chocolates, or among other things, my specially ground Italian coffee? Of course I'll have to take artificial sweeteners, and some of that stuff they make bread out of. Yes...flour. I'm okay at making pancakes...did it once for a dare.

Alcohol is banned they said. I'll hide a few bottles in my backpack.

Move Over James Bond

My personal beauty items will have to be curtailed — a problem. I'd like to take everything. They cost me a fortune. But I'll have to settle for a bag or two containing cosmetics for all occasions, body beautiful treatments, hair lotions, hand-made soap...my sunnies of course – and the specially prepared sun cream for my sensitive skin.

Choosing clothes and shoes will be more than a two-day decision-making effort. Some cupboards I haven't looked in for ages. They said the weather is cold and hot, like earth. I'll take the winter underwear I bought for that trip to Alaska and never wore. It snowed so I never went out of the guesthouse, but neither did most of the men. It was great. I must put in a cocktail frock or two...you never know. They'll have to have some form of entertainment, which means light refreshments – oysters, cheese, crackers and other mixed party food are a necessity. In they'll go.

There's my designer label sportswear...can't leave them behind. What would I exercise in? They must have a gym. I'll also include a pair of designer joggers in the unlikely event that I'm forced to walk on dirt. Oh! I can't leave my high heels behind...I'd die in sexless flatties.

'Simple nightwear as you may be sharing,' they said. Not me! Anyway I have no such thing...only lace two-piece, and see-throughs – my ex loved those – and I may be lucky. I'll also include a gown for chilly nights. A doona wouldn't go amiss. No! Too big. Anyway, I can always find someone to keep me warm. I make friends easily.

They tell us there'll be plenty of eating utensils, so not to bother. Horror of horrors – I refuse to eat off common people's stuff. You never know these days. I'll sneak in my good china...heavens no...it'll be stolen by some low life. I'll hide it and take the Wedgwood, and perhaps a see-through saucepan or two. The smell of a frozen soup mix simmering on the stovetop provides a good homely background on a first date. I've tried it, but it's not something you actually eat.

What did they say about light? I can't remember. I'll act as I would when there's a local blackout. I'll put in torches, batteries, radio, and cassette player. They'll fit somewhere. Of course I'll have to leave behind all the bulky items like the television. What will I do without my computer and my exercise bike, but some nice gentleman rich enough to bypass the rules, is sure to have some. As I already mentioned, I make friends easily.

I'll miss family and friends. A couple of photo albums wouldn't take up very much space, plus that pile of love letters from my ex. They've been good for a laugh, or at times a tear or two

....

I arrived at the terminal at the allocated time and day struggling with a backpack, two bursting overnight bags, plus a large handbag – thank goodness for wheels – and regretting I'd left piles of necessities behind. There were no porters so I was forced to drag my own belongings up to the counter. I'll put in an official complaint later.

Those dreadful men unceremoniously took my bags one by one and emptied the contents on to their desks…so embarrassing!

'EXCUSE ME!' I kept saying. They ignored me.

'Can't take all that lady,' the burly official muttered.

But…!'

They gloatingly pounced on my six bottles of wine. I argued over keeping at least one. 'I'll need that,' I told them sweetly as I hugged the two biggest bottles against my chest. They relented, and then went on to push piles of other items to one side, but the tins of best brand fish, cocktail snacks, and the pile of Weight Watchers meals went unchecked.

A quick swift body search by a leering officer who concentrated mostly on my thighs, although not a 'wandering hands' type thank goodness, lost interest when he noticed a younger very pretty girl was next in line. So my favourite jade and ruby jewellery, for luck and love, remained hidden behind the elastic in my panties, undiscovered. I was pleased I'd turned some of my money into gold, hidden in the padding of my bra. I looked several sizes bigger there, but who's to know? Gold is the best form of currency anywhere, and if it isn't on Mars they'll soon make it the main one

'Life is so hard when you have to go without the necessaries of life,' I told the men and they did weaken after I parted with financial inducement – I was clever to remember to bring the cash I had hidden in the wall safe to avoid tax. They allowed me to keep a lot of forbidden items, like my coffee beans, slimming tablets, body lotions and other essential beauty items, and the mass of jewellery I was wearing. They also allowed me to keep the torches, batteries, and the radio – probably can't get anything on it there anyway. Other things I retained were the sun hat, track suits, several changes of light and heavy underwear, light dresses, two joggers, two pairs of revolting low-heeled shoes, slacks and tops, plus one saucepan, but had to say goodbye to one overnight bag full of cosmetics, and hand-made organic beauty aids – all good for the environment though who worries now?

He told me that shiploads of goods were on their way there and we'll be able to get what we wanted after they arrived. I'm not sure I trust him, especially when I caught him winking at his assistant as I was being dismissed.

I walked off laden with my remaining luggage. When the heavy doors of the ship slammed and squeaked shut behind me, I was delighted I had saved one photo album and my deceased mother's last gift to me – a set of crocheted doilies made by her own hand in the olden days. I had also fought and won to keep my porcelain doll 'Shara' that I had from childhood – my only link to my past. I held 'Shara' close, felt very alone and cried, spoiling my make-up.

....

FROM THE LATEST NEWS REPORTS BACK ON EARTH:

Channel 2 has to advise that the first passenger ship to Mars, severely over-crowded, has crashed on the far side of Mars. No survivors have been found, but Marcia's diary and other personal items belonging to many of the passengers have been located. Searches are still continuing for any likely survivors but officials offer little hope of finding anyone alive.

A second passenger ship leave for Mars on Monday week.

MOVE OVER JAMES BOND: ASSIGNMEENT 2

"SO GOOD TO TALK TO SOMEONE NOT STONED out of their brain." I told Mr Grant Stand, my C.E.O. who was only paying me a visit in person because he was so short-staffed.

I, Mal Murphy, real name Ernest Moneylove under-cover member of the Drug Squad met my Chief on this rearranged half-bush-hidden bench in a neighbourhood park. This was necessary because I could not be seen fraternising with ordinary people outside the derelict and drug-taking group I had infiltrated or I could blow my cover.

The Chief, already having eyed my unshaven face, long hair, grubby clothes and dirty boots with distaste was seated at the far end of the park bench. I sat at the other. He also held a handkerchief to his face as the wind was not being sociable. We did not look at each other when we spoke.

"Let's not stay too long Ernest, or rather Mal. What have you got on the drug boss...the General?" He spoke crisply. "You should be close. You've been mixing with that low life long enough. Don't mess it up this time."

I ignored that, as my idol James Bond of movie fame would have, and replied. "Shouldn't be long. I've an appointment with the local supplier, Bull. He's been named Bull. It's short for bull terrier. He's called that because he never lets go of a client, unless they've died or they're broke. It's for tonight at 10 pm at the boarding house I've moved into. His room's across from mine. The plan is to find out who the General is. It will be a cinch after I record Bull selling me drugs and giving me other incriminating information."

"How did you get on to this ...er...Bull?" The chief leaned forward with interest

"Through a half-dead junkie called 'Lucky'. He told me where the drug dealer lived so I moved in there too."

"Can you trust a junkie?"

"I just had to take the gamble."

The Chief was pleased. I could tell from his expression, even though he gruffly said, 'Bout' time too. You've been months on the streets and yet you haven't come up with any firm leads until now, hopefully. At today's briefing session it was suggested, that as you seemed to be getting nowhere, you should be replaced – new blood, new angle. Johnny Smith's name came up. Nothing personal you understand."

I resented the inference that I had failed my assignment, and was not surprised if backstabbing Johnny would be in behind it somewhere, trying to take the glory, after all my work.

"I need a little more time," I said, more to convince him than myself, after all, my plan was foolproof. I had a James Bond grasp on it. "I'll be able to give you names tonight."

"Okay…if not, we'll meet here same time tomorrow, but you'd better come up with the goods soon."

"You'll have them. After tonight we should be able to close in."

We parted, each in opposite directions. No need for 'goodbyes.'

I thought about what he said. For three months I had been on the streets, mixing with drug addicts and derelicts. I'd like to see jealous Johnny take that on. I was living in a rundown guesthouse, unshaven most of the time, and with clothes needing a good wash or a trip to the rubbish bin. The idea of giving up and going home to Estella and our nerve and body-soothing waterbed was temptation personified. Although I had nothing concrete as yet, I, Ernest Moneylove, like James Bond, never give up. Tonight was the break I had been waiting and planning for. Soon I'll be up there at the top with James.

It was 9.30 pm when I arrived back at the guesthouse. Not knowing whether or not I was being watched, I staggered a bit and mumbled away to myself as I made my way up the stairs and inside. There was no one in the passageway so I sidled up to Bull's room. I was 'casing the joint' as they say. I staggered sideways so I could put my ear closer to the door. Doors and walls in this old building were thin. If he was not alone it meant he had suspicions about me, his new customer, and a reception committee could be waiting. If so it would be 'curtains' for me.

All was silence in his room, except for the clank of a bottle on a table, the clinking of several glasses and the sound of them being filled. I smiled, but hoped these were not in advance of my visit. I always insist on mine being 'shaken not stirred' as James Bond likes it, but one has to suffer sometimes in this job. What it did show was that I was going to be treated as a guest to soften me up, probably to discover where I got my 'present supply', and whether that someone had moved into his territory. I had played my cards right so far.

I heard footsteps coming up the front stairs. I moved quickly away and into my own room. I had to watch every move in case I had unwittingly blown my cover. Through a narrow opening of my door I watched to see who was coming. It was Kandy, a well-known ageing prostitute and drug addict who worked the streets near by. Her red dyed, long hair, drawn back in a bun with fancy clips, was a pathetic attempt to look younger. She stared unblinking, from glazed eyes heavily outlined with makeup. Perspiration glistened on her forehead and she shivered as if cold. No gamble as to where she was heading.

She knocked three times at intervals on Bull's door. *She must be desperate for a fix to risk visiting Bull uninvited, unless the drinks are for her but I doubt that.* I knew from what Mad Molly, who rented the room adjoining Bull's, told me in bits and pieces, mostly through her eternal reciting of nursery rhymes, that anyone without enough cash for drugs was in for a rough time with Bull. Everyone around the streets knew Kandy was having trouble attracting customers.

I retreated to my room and stretched out on the hard springless bed to await the sound of her footsteps in the passageway as she left Bull's room.

I unwittingly fell asleep. A singsong voice, loud over the sound of rushing water from the bathroom next door woke me. It was Mad Molly at it again. She was singing a nursery rhyme in a high-pitched tone. This time it was 'Twinkle twinkle little star. How I wonder what you are...' She was emphasising the 'How I wonder what you are...' line over and over. *Is she on to me?* An agent has to stay alert and read between the lines.

I recalled that when I first arrived she was sweeping the passageway and wiping doorknobs. She was wearing gloves and I discovered she wore them constantly, even when she went to the common bathroom. I remember going up to this tiny, frail woman and introducing myself

"Hello, I'm Mal Murphy – room 19. I'm new here." She had turned her wrinkled face up at me as she sucked in her lips between her toothless gums. In a squeaky voice she began reciting. 'Simple Simon met a pieman going to the fair. Simple Simon wants some pie. Are you Simple Simon?" She croaked and I knew it was her laugh. As I got to know her I gleaned from lines she emphasised that she knew when Bull had visitors. I believed she had a clear idea of what went on in his room.

It was obvious to me that she was not like the rest of us, so I smiled and walked away. After that we were sort of friends. I was the only one she gave that grin. I believed she was not as silly as she made out and could be a source of information, so several times I took her for an ice cream at the corner shop and called her 'sister'.

Fully awake now I pulled out my Rolex watch from the depth of my deep pants' pocket. It was close to midnight. Cursing, I decided to go to Bull's room anyway. I figured that Kandy would have left by now. I hoped I had not blown it and would have to think up some excuse to give him for being late.

I could picture the Chief's face if I told him, 'I had this wonderful opportunity to bag the General and his cronies but I fell asleep.' I would never live it down and be off the team quick smart and my work rival Smithy would somersault with joy.

I hurried to his door. To my surprise it was open. I looked around. When I saw no one in the passageway I entered the room. What I saw stopped me in my tracks and a shiver ran down my spine. I'd never seen dead people before. I think they were dead. Bull was stretched out on his back on the floor with a knife in his chest. An empty glass lay beside him. Kandy was lying not far from him.

I felt sick and stared at the ceiling until my stomach settled down. My special training and devotion to James Bond films then took over. I stiffened and listened intently. Was someone still lurking in the room? The bathroom door was ajar but it was empty. There was nowhere else where anyone could hide. If anyone else was involved they would be long gone.

What a lucky break.

I went through Bull's pockets, taking receipts but ignored his wallet. I searched his desk drawers and found a diary and papers with names, numbers and supplies. Some were in code but that would not be hard for headquarters to break. I quietly slipped out of the building, unseen I thought, to a public phone and telephoned the Chief.

"I knew you **might** do it." He sounded approving for once. "Looks like you've come up with the goods after all. I'll have our undercover courier pick them up. We have work to do." He sounded so excited you would have thought he had carried out this investigation all by himself. I was 'on a high' myself and wanted to leave immediately.

"I can't wait to be in my own bed tonight, between clean sheets, with Estella."

"I know you must be impatient, but stay put. Leaving might attract police suspicion and spoil everything." He quickly hung up before I could argue with him. Half an hour later the courier, who was Smithy, arrived. He was dressed like a bloke down on his luck, with old baggy clothes, worn hat and shoes but all spotless – a clean giveaway – but when he gave me the right password I handed over the papers.

I could sleep peacefully now my assignment was almost over. Soon I'd be home, perhaps by tonight. I waited for the chief's order. To celebrate my near release I poured myself a drink – shaken not stirred as James Bond likes it.

Later I was surprised by a knock on the door. When I opened it two police officers stood there – investigating Bull's murder no doubt. They looked me over, from my unshaven face down to my worn dirty boots, then back to my face. Their expressions were one of contempt and disgust. Obviously they believed they were seeing another 'no-hoper'.

"Yeah?" I enquired, yawning.

"We are investigation the demise of a male and female in this building."

"Who?" I tried to look surprised, and shocked.

"Mr. Wall and a female whom we believe was known as Kandy."

"Who? You mean the Bull?" They stared at me intently. "The Bull, that's what he's called around here. Didn't know he had a girlfriend though. He was no friend of mine."

They made no comment and went on, "Perhaps you can help us in our investigation. Have you any idea why this Kandy woman would want to kill Mr. Wall and then herself?"

"Naw...seen them around but that's all."

"Did you see any strangers, or anyone from here acting suspicious last night?"

I tried to look puzzled. "No," I said, "I can't help you."

"If you remember anything that might help let us know." He dropped his card on the table. He did not want to get too close to me.

"I sure will," I lied.

They looked me up and down again as they left. One muttered, 'Fat chance.'

I stretched out again on the unyielding mattress. I was bored and anxiously waiting for the call that said the squad had nabbed the General. If the raids had been carried out in the early hours of the morning I should be home by the afternoon. I waited impatiently, growing more anxious as the time dragged on. I tried to concentrate on picturing the chief giving me a promotion and perhaps a medal, until I dozed off from boredom.

I jumped to awareness when a loud knock came on my door.

'I'm home and hosed,' I thought, but was dismayed to find the two police officers standing there. I stared blankly at them.

"You are Mal Murphy?"

"Yes, but I thought you knew that."

"We have been advised that you were seen near Mr. Wall's door around midnight. There are stains on the floor, which lead back to this room. We would like to examine the shoes you were wearing last night."

My heart sank. In my haste I had been careful but obviously not careful enough. I had overlooked checking my shoes and also forgotten Molly, who knew everything that went on.

"If Mad Molly told you anything I wouldn't take it seriously. She's not called Mad Molly for nothing."

"Perhaps...after saying she saw you go into Bull's room she did recite Humpty Dumpy had a great fall...but...your shoes."

The officers were watching me closely as I dragged them from under the bed. They put on gloves and gingerly turned them over. Both looked suspiciously at several stains on the soles – something that I had failed to notice. I will make a note of that in my diary for future reference.

"This could be blood. We'd like you to come with us to the station while these are being examined."

I had no choice but to go with them.

In the Station's interview room I was told to sit and wait, but after some time of being ignored I put my own question to the two detectives watching me. No doubt they were making certain I did not leave before they were ready to dismiss me.

"I didn't do anything so why am I here?"

"You probably know already." He gave a twist of his lips. "Mr. Wall did not die from a stab wound. The knife blade was too short and slipped off his rib cage...plenty of blood but not serious. And, he did not die from the hit on the head sustained when he fell. He died from poison."

"Poison!" I did not have to pretend surprise. It was genuine. I suddenly remembered the empty glass I had seen on the carpet beside Bull.

"Have you anything to add. Any information you would like to get off your chest as to what you were doing in Mr Wall's room at midnight."

"No sir," I replied.

A phone rang and one officer left and closed the door behind him. There was silence until he returned half an hour later. He wore a satisfied smirk. "Perhaps you would like to change your story about last night. Your shoes show blood, fresh

Move Over James Bond

blood on both. Will we find it once belonged to Mr Wall?"

Although he spoke light-heartedly, as if he was my friend and confidant, I was up to that trick. The stern expression in his eyes showed a man who got the answers he wanted, given time.

"I don't know anything officer."

"Well we're arresting you on suspicion of murder."

"But I had nothing to do with it." I protested loudly, as I realised I may not be home by dark. I needed help. *Stay cool like James Bond.*

"May I use the 'phone sir?"

"One call only. If it's to a lawyer I doubt whether any lawyer would come within miles of you until you're deloused."

I called Estella. She sounded pleased to hear my voice. I think.

"Don't be alarmed, but I have met with a minor set-back." The listening police officer smiled. "I've been arrested on suspicion of murder." There was silence at the other end and I thought I heard suppressed laughter – probably from the TV. "Of course it's a mistake. No, I haven't messed up. Will you get on to you-know-who to straighten it out so I can be home tonight?"

"Are you sure, very sure, everything will be all right?" Now she sounded fed-up. Our relationship was getting shakier by the minute, but as a fan of James Bond I could soon remedy that.

"Of course, no sweat, I'll be home tonight...bye...love you."

The listening officer was grinning now. I wanted to punch him so hard he would not grin for a week.

I was confident that the Chief would have me out shortly, but I waited, and waited. I endured more questioning from the police who appeared convinced they had the goods on me. 'Robbery – for drugs or for drug money – gone wrong' would be the conclusion I expected they would make. The cards were stacked against me. *What's holding up the Chief?*

After a nightmarish almost sleepless twenty-four hours in a cold cell with several snoring drunks, Smithy, now in a business suit, arrived to bail me out. *Estella must have got the message to the*

Chief, but what took them so long?

"You're free for the moment," was the Sergeant's parting words. "And don't leave your present address. Report back here next Monday for an interview, if we don't pick you up before then."

At the door I skipped a few steps, landing on the footpath. I ran to catch up with the now mysteriously acting Smithy but he had disappeared. He must have been told not to wait around, but why? I was beginning to worry as I returned to the guesthouse to pack. I wanted to ring the Chief to find out if they had arrested the General, but I may have been followed so I held myself back. All I could do was wait until the Chief let the police know I was an undercover drug squad member. Until then I would remain under suspicion.

With plenty of time to think, I began to wonder if the Chief had forgotten me in the excitement. He showed he was not too concerned about the strain between Estella and myself over this assignment. It had been a long stint for us both, combined with the rising impatience at headquarters to get results. I put these doubts down to frustration and tried to dismiss them but they still stayed, hovering in the background of my brain.

I walked back and forth for what seemed the thousandth time when a knock came on the door. I jumped, then run to the door, excited. 'At last!' I thought.

I swung the door open. My face dropped. It was mad Molly. "Sorry you got arrested." Molly was in one of her rare talking moods.

"That's all right...no harm done." Then it dawned on me. "You were on walkabout too. Bull's door should not have been open. What did you see?"

"Tomato sauce."

"Tomato sauce? Oh, of course, tomato sauce... blood ... so you had a look?"

"Humpty dumpty sat on a wall, humpty dumpty had a great fall. All the king's horses and all the king's men couldn't put humpty together again . . ."

So Bull was humpty dumpty. I had to learn more. "Like an

ice-cream?" I asked.

She took my arm with one of her gloved hands. I brought the ice creams at the corner store and we ate them sitting on the front steps.

"What did you see Molly?"

"Humpty, dumpty sat on a wall . . ."

I interrupted her flow. "You saw Mr. Hall. He's humpy dumpy isn't he, with his big round tummy and he had a great fall. Of course, you saw the woman too, didn't you?"

"Asleep she was – sleeping beauty. He was moaning. I think he was thirsty so I gave him a drink from a glass on the table. Humpty Dumpy sat on a wall, humpty dumpty had a great fal . . . no one can put him together again."

I realised that was how he got poisoned. When Bull poured the drinks, the one that he laced with slow poison must have been for me. I would have been back in my room before it took effect. I must have somehow blown my cover. Obviously he had been told of my meeting with the Chief. He was ready if something I said convinced him I was not genuine. *It was that drug addict, Lucky! You can't trust anyone.* I was horrified to think that I could have been dead instead of those ill-fated two.

"You're a darling Molly." I rose to leave. As I stood up a swaying apparently drunken man bumped against me. He slipped a note into my pocket.

'Ring Chief,' was all it said, but that was enough to tell me that the operation had been successful – no more secret meetings in parks. No more nights away from Estella.

I hurried to the street-corner telephone. I would have run but a running derelict would attract unwanted attention.

The Chief answered immediately, which surprised me. He probably thought it was the press wanting an interview.

"Mad Molly was the one who gave Bull the poison by accident, but don't bring her into it. Anyway, she always wears gloves." I then blurted out the whole story. He heard me and then to my annoyance said, "I really didn't think you did it." He seemed to be smiling.

"Thanks." I hoped I sounded pleased not sarcastic.

"By the way that prostitute died of a heart attack while on a mixture of drugs. Now for the best news. The 'General' and his cronies have been arrested." His self-satisfaction was evident in his voice.

"Great. Have you got on to the police? I can't wait to get home."

"All done, and the police have concluded it was murder and death by misadventure. Case closed."

"I'll come and see you tomorrow about a rise in my pay."

"Like hell you will." The Chief laughed and hung up.

One hour later I was home with Estella. She would not come near me until after an all over bodily clean up. Then after we made our exhausting 'good to be together again' demonstrations until exhausted, we seated ourselves very close while waiting for the T.V. news to come on. I was excited and could hardly sit still, much to Estella's annoyance.

It was the 'news of the day' on all channels.

I leaned forward when the Chief, looking very self-satisfied began to give a run-down on how they had achieved this dangerous drug bust. I waited breathless, to hear myself mentioned as he gave details of the arrest of the General and the disbanding of his organisation. To my disgust he added that it was the fine work of his men that made it possible. *MEN? ME! It was ME that did it all.* Then I nearly choked when I saw that crawler Johnny was standing near the Chief and grinning madly as if he was the one who had done all the dirty work.

James Bond, that successful arch-spy and ladies' man never had to contend with such glory seekers like Smithy undermining him. *If only I had his equipment…hmmm.*

WHEN THE WORST COMES TO THE WORST

"WE'RE ALL HERE in the front yard near the fountain like I asked you to, so's we can work out a plan of escape when the worst comes to the worst, which could be any day now." announced ex-army Doug, the self-appointed leader of the group.

"Yes, and I want to be prepared. Shouldn't we at least be ready with our rubber duckies," put forward John.

"Keep him quiet will you?"

John received several digs in his ribs. He shrugged. "Just trying to be helpful."

"Rubber duckies indeed! When the high surges of water come hurling down we need more than rubber duckies – unless they're army ducks."

"I think it was a good idea of John's to bring it up anyway," stammered John's would-be girlfriend, Elsie.

"Why are there only a handful of us? I thought we'd have a crowd seeing everyone will be effected, so, where are they?"

"Buying up homes in Toowoomba I reckon. It's the closest mountain-top city."

"Is it a silly question to ask? Why aren't we up there?"

"Because they didn't think about us that's why. They never do," ventured Betty

"I got a scooter for Christmas. I could leave now," someone said.

"You wouldn't make the climb up the mountain…too much for your right leg," commented another, who was ignored.

"We just have to decide the best way to save ourselves. We have to be ready WHEN it happens, " stated Doug emphatically.

"What about those people who's still in their houses? I can see lights on in some of them," Horace said as his arm swept the buildings below.

"They're probably discussing an escape route right now like us, or they're unbelievers, or, they have a death wish or something, but it's all true. It was on TV."

"God wouldn't let it happen." Maize searched for her rosary

beads as she spoke.

Doug looked down at her and said kindly. "He made one flood so he's had practice. Besides all the pollies have left. I saw them on TV in their cars going somewhere...must've been going to Toowoomba or that other high spot, Montville. That tells you something doesn't it?"

"What?"

"Never mind... It's every man...Okay Olive, put your hand down. Keep your woman's lib stuff to yourself, I meant woman too. All right, for himself, for herself, okay? My suggestion is to find a high building like next-door and go to the top and stay there till it's back to normal. They don't last for ever."

"What if they won't let us?"

Pete stepped forward. "We could ask the caretaker for the key. He knows me."

"Excellent suggestion Pete. That's your job. Any other suggestions?"

"What about boats? Could we get some now, so we're ready in case Pete can't get the key? My legs are too far gone to walk all the way up the Toowoomba range."

"I'd have to look into that, but my guess is the moneyed lot would have commandeered them...you know what those grabbers are like...but...if there were any left we might be able to get some. That's your job Wallis. You were a sea faring man."

"Gee! Thanks."

"Where are you ladies going?"

"To get our raincoats."

"Don't be silly. Stay here. We're not ready yet. We're only getting a plan into action, but keep them handy in case."

A booming voice shouted out from behind them. "Folks!"

They turned as one towards the uniformed man standing in the doorway of the building behind them.

"What you all out here for? It's getting dark."

"We're deciding what we're going to do when the floods come. We want to be prepared. That ozone layer thing's causing it."

"I'm going to buy a raincoat. I've got an umbrella," said May and the other ladies nodded as they all moved towards the door.

"Can we buy a boat now...just to be ready?" spoke up Wallis.

"We'll have to look into that one," was Doug's response.

The man beside Doug smiled and said, 'If it's what you saw on T.V. the other night about the poles melting and flooding the earth, you've got plenty of time... it's not expected for another hundred years or so."

"That's what they say, but they may be wrong, and we're got to be ready," asserted Doug.

"Worry about it tomorrow. Right now, tea's ready," he announced.

"Are you sure about the hundred years?" queried Doug.

"I swear," was the reply.

As the fear disappeared the subject was dropped, and forgotten. They began discussing the possible dinner menu.

"I'm hungry," announced Olive

"Me too," echoed Bill.

"I hope it's chicken. I like chicken," said Maisie.

"I hate soup," muttered Jean.

As they reached the dining room the Matron was frowning at them. "Tea's ready and you're keeping the staff back. This nursing home hasn't got extra money to pay overtime. Just hurry yourselves a little more.' They keep chatting and did not appear to have heard her.

The Matron glanced to the ceiling as she commenced to follow.

WAGES OF SIN

BERT BARRETT STOPPED SPEAKING. In the silence that followed, Bert's eighty-year-old body rocked back and forth in the ancient creaking rocking chair on the front verandah of his small century-old worker's cottage. His small piercing eyes concentrated their gaze on his worried daughter while his long thin fingers gripped the carved arms of the chair spasmodically. In the lull, the clapping of the rocking chair's arched legs and the creaking of the loose floorboards were so monotonous the sound jarred on Margaret's nerves.

She was balancing her trim, suited body on the end of the long wooden stool her father had built in the early days of his marriage, when furniture was hard to come by and money the same, and hoped her father would see reason.

Bert spoke again but in an even sterner voice. "I've told you I don't want anything to do with this million dollars you tell me I've won. It's gambling, and gambling's a sin."

His thin voice began to rise as Margaret had heard it many times when, as a lay preacher he had delivered his many sermons. 'Gambling is a sin and 'the wages of sin' are death!' was a favourite topic of his. Now he spat the words at her again.

The familiar stubborn set of his jutting chin made his daughter aware that she would have to be more persuasive. She leaned forward in silence, patiently listening to her father repeat himself over and over again. Her mind drifted and his words began to float over her without response.

In the background, she could hear faithful old Alice the housekeeper rattling crockery in her arthritic hands. She hoped that afternoon tea would soon be ready. As her father's voice had become louder and shriller, she knew he felt his message was no longer reaching her consciousness. In a nervous gesture she brushed her dark brown hair with its streaks of grey, back from her forehead, and waited for him to finish.

"Gambling's a sin. If the good Lord wanted me to have a million dollars he'd have given it to me through hard work," he told her again, nodding his head sharply several times to emphasise his point. He then paused to regain his breath, still agitated. Margaret silently waited. She knew that to interrupt would not stop him finishing what he wanted to say.

Once again Bert leaned forward, staring with unblinking eyes into hers – eyes that were narrow slits above hollow cheeks and thin almost disappearing lips.

"Why did old Alice buy me a ticket in the lotto anyway? I never asked her. I don't need the money. I've got everything I want. The house may have seen better days but it'll see me out." Leaning forward and directing his gaze upwards towards the galvanised iron roof overhead he continued loudly, "No good can come of it you'll see. There's bad days ahead."

He looked to his daughter for a response as he melted his thin frame back into the contours of his chair. He wore the satisfied expression of someone making a strong declaration of their convictions. He received no response. Margaret was gratefully listening to the dull thud of plates being clumsily placed on the well-scrubbed wooden kitchen table inside. Knowing Alice was nearly ready for them, she rose, ready to help her father from his chair.

"Alice has looked after you for fifteen years, ever since Mum died," she said, "so why not give some of your winnings to Alice and to us. Your grandkids have to be educated you know. We could all do with some help."

Bert snorted. "Alice, at eighty-six? What would she want money for? Anyway I have to claim it first and I won't be doing any such thing," he grunted. "Take my word for it, no good will come of it you see. Pastor John said only last Sunday that to gamble is to bring the wrath of the Lord down upon you. You just wait and see my girl." He paused. "You know I'm right."

Margaret well knew that when her father forecast doom it was better to be patiently silent.

Bert, from years of rigid habit on both his and Alice's part, knew instinctively it was time for afternoon tea. He did not have to wait for her to call him. He gripped the arms of his chair and had risen to his feet when a loud wail from the garden filled the air. Alice's black cat chased by the grey tomcat from the next-door dwelling ran howling from among the hibiscus bushes. It took the three weather-worn steps in one leap to land close to Bert's feet, then with one bound disappeared into the house.

The shock of the sudden event made Bert topple backwards into his chair, which responded by rocking vigorously, it's rough thick legs slapping the uneven floor with savage noisy clouts.

"You see, you see, I haven't even touched the money and it's started! I could have been killed." He was shouting now and his voice came in breathless bursts.

"There, there," soothed Margaret, stroking his back, "no harm done."

She helped the shaking man to rise. Together they went into the house.

In the kitchen they sat across from one another at the old heavy wooden table; its scratches and stains hidden beneath a white starched linen tablecloth.

Margaret, always happy in Alice's company, watched Alice busy herself at the stove. Her round jolly face and plump body made an almost comical contrast to Bert's frowning face and thin body.

"Takes ages to boil the water on the wood stove. The wood's damp. I hope you get one of those electric ones now you're rich," Alice suggested...her voice high pitched and excited.

"Huh!" grunted Bert dismissing the subject.

Having more than usual shaky hands Alice poured their tea. She placed the plate of biscuits conveniently close to both Bert and Margaret before sinking slowly into her chair. In the immediate silence that followed Margaret heard her groan. She looked up from her teacup. Alice's face was taking on a strained, pained expression as her rosy face drained of colour. Shocked, they both watched it turn into a grey mask.

"Don't feel well," she whispered as her podgy hand went to her chest.

As they watched with surprise and creeping horror she slid to the floor, unconscious. Margaret rushed to Alice's aid but could do nothing. It was too late.

Bert sat stunned. Dr Brady arrived, confirmed Alice could

not be saved, and took over the necessary arrangements. Margaret, in shock herself, was fearful for her aged father. At her request Dr Brady gave him a sedative. Bert kept protesting and repeating, "The wages of sin are death. It's happened. It's happened."

"The shock of the win on her bad heart got the best of her. But she had a good long life and was active to the end," explained Doctor Brady in his effort to comfort both Bert and Margaret.

"You see, you see," spluttered Bert – the sedative not yet taking effect. "I'll be next, and I haven't even taken the money."

"What nonsense! Stop talking like that." Margaret was now becoming impatient with him. "Al's transfer has come through and we'll be leaving in three days for Brisbane. I want to know before I go that you're being well looked after, so I'll ring the employment agency and find you a temporary housekeeper."

The following day Margaret interviewed a young, attractive, dark haired woman who claimed she was a divorcee. Margaret viewed her excellent reference. It was written on the letterhead of a property situated in some remote part of West Australia. Although Margaret thought it strange for this young stylish woman from a busy place like Amsterdam to bury herself in the outback, she watched Greta immediately begin to treat her father in a motherly fashion. Margaret watched in amazement at her father's beaming response in smiles and 'Oh thank you's' to Greta's flattery and attention. It seemed to be making the old man feel young again, even if he was acting out of character for his age.

Although sensing some disquiet that she could not pinpoint, Margaret was satisfied that, if Greta continued in this manner, it would probably be good for her father. She emphasised to Greta that it was only a temporary appointment until she got back. Greta smiled charmingly and said, "Of course I understand. I'll see you then. Don't worry about your father. He's in good hands." Margaret kissed her father goodbye and carried with her a niggling doubt about her choice of housekeeper.

Before leaving, Dr Brady promised to talk sense into Bert about the million dollars he had won, and Margaret, having to be satisfied with that, left for home.

Packing, unpacking and settling into her new home took longer than Margaret expected so she was unable to make another five-hour trip to visit her father as she had promised. She knew he would not telephone her as he refused to have one in the house, and nothing could persuade him to use one elsewhere.

'New-fangled contraptions. Didn't need it before, don't need it now,' was his stubborn refusal when approached on the subject.

Time passed and when Dr Brady, who had promised to keep her informed, had not contacted her, she at first felt no news was good news. However, when more days passed she became worried. Nervously she telephoned Dr. Brady.

"Why hello Margaret. I have been meaning to 'phone you. Your father did come to see me. I promised to ring you but I became so busy. But to get back to your father. You know how he, well, was so religious?"

Past events flashed through Margaret's mind. Yes, she knew all too well. She managed to gulp, "So?" From the tone in his voice she now feared the worst. Her heart pondered with dismay as she waited for him to continue.

"Well, he told me that his new housekeeper believed as he did. She quoted the Bible to him, and she seemed to have an answer for everything. She convinced him that like Moses, God was testing his faith by giving him a million dollars."

"Faith? But what about the wages of sin being death thing he goes on with?" interrupted Margaret.

"He stopped quoting that one after Greta persuaded him that it was poor Alice who paid the ultimate price for buying the ticket. She convinced him that no blame could be laid on him. Finally she persuaded him to claim the money and when a bolt of lightning did not strike him down, and I'm quoting him here, she sweetly told him that it was God's will to take the win. God's will that he use it to help mankind. He mentioned things like, 'If you have two coats give one to another', and so forth and...."

Dr Brady's voice trailed off. Margaret sensed bad news.

"Well, what happened? Is he alright?" she demanded, now

really convinced that something dreadful had happened.

"Well, err," slowly continued Dr Brady, who was obviously reluctant to continue. "Well, err . . . the next thing Bert told me was that he, with Greta's assistance, would cast bread upon the waters so to speak, by helping others worse off. Although I think the only good Greta would do in this world would be to keep people in employment in expensive tourist resorts and shops."

Margaret felt faint and her knuckles were white as she clutched the telephone pressed hard against her ear. She waited, thinking, 'When I met her I sensed something very wrong about her...a gold digger, of course! It's all my fault. I should have known...checked her out more.'

As there was a sudden silence at her end Dr Brady asked anxiously, "Are you all right Margaret?"

Margaret swallowed. She pictured her father sitting in his rocking chair now lonely and completely alone, and Greta with his million dollars off somewhere spending it. She would have to go to him immediately.

"Yes I'm all right, but how is father? Obviously Greta's left."

"Well, err...not exactly. Your father is with Greta somewhere in Asia by now on a world cruise. Bert said they'd be back in two months and to tell Margaret not to worry."

"Not to worry!" screeched Margaret, "What a stupid thing to say! My poor father in his old age and dotage, being led astray by a gold digger fifty odd years his junior. She has to be stopped. I want her arrested. I want my poor father back home where he belongs. I want you to examine him to decide whether he is capable of looking after himself and whether he should have twenty-four hour care . . . perhaps in a nursing home . . ."

"Hold on Margaret. There's more. The sad news is that your father has a very bad heart and cancer. He told me not to tell you. 'God's will,' he said. Unfortunately, any great excitement could cause a fatal collapse. I am afraid that your father has, at the most, twelve months left.

"Oh that's terrible, but I did know he was ill. Alice told me but I put it to the back of my mind. Is it possible he could collapse on the trip?"

"If he does, arrangements have been made for his immediate return."

Margaret pictured Greta over-exciting her father, sending him home and going on to spend all his money." Bitter tears welled up in her eyes and anger filled her heart. "He must be brought home immediately. I will not be happy until he's home and that gold digger dealt with and...."

Dr Brady interrupted.

"There is some thing else. Before he left he asked for my advice about claiming the money. At my insistence he also made his will. He left whatever is left of his win to you and your family. He said something about the grandchildren could do with some."

"What? Well he did the right thing. He is a very clever sensible man and although he is old he has not lost any of his mental powers. I suppose Greta ends up with a slice though," she added bitterly.

"Well, not actually – not a cent. If anything happens to him she's left high and dry, with only the free trip to remember your father for."

Margaret held back a laugh of delight and satisfaction.

"What a clever man my father is. What did he say about the wages of sin are death bit?"

"He said, If the wages of sin are death then to die in Greta's arms would be God working in mysterious ways."

THE END OF PEGGY-DAN

JUDY DRUMMED THE FINGERS OF HER LEFT HAND on the table while she impatiently waited for her friend Dora to answer her mobile at her end. She knew Dora, who had arrived that morning from her six months trip abroad, would be busy unpacking, but this was urgent, before the results of the misery from her loss overwhelmed her again.

The burring sound finally stopped. "Hullo? Dora? Is that you?" came Judy's demand.

"Yes, of course it is. What's the matter Judy? You sound upset. You've been crying haven't you?"

"Something awful has happened. Remember I promised to tell you all about my pet Peggy-Dan that I got just after you left, when we met tomorrow. Well I can't now. Peggy-Dan's DEAD. John killed PD! I can't tell you how. It would only upset me even more to describe it."

"You poor darling. You must be devastated. You've always wanted a pet."

Judy began to whine. "I wish I had hidden my precious pet in the garage somewhere before John in a fit of temper got…rid of it. It shouldn't have died young." Judy could not halt the tears. "It should still be alive. You know John always says, 'NO pets,' whenever I bring up the subject. 'We don't need any smelly, demanding items of no worth around the place. We have each other darling. That's all we need.' But, as you know I've always had a pet. Well, before John that is…from when I was a kid. If we had a child it would be different, but John insists on waiting, and waiting…financial reasons and all that… poor PD."

"You told me that if you got a pet you would hide it away from John, so he wouldn't know anything about it."

"I was too busy and forgot. Oh Dora! I miss Peggy-Dan. I miss the cocky look of expectancy whenever it knew I was making breakfast. If John was still home I would wave it back, and it would hide in the sink cupboard. It liked the warmth there I think. Then it would come out, get up on the table and I would drop little titbits off the side of my plate for it. Life will never be the same."

"Judy have you thought? I mean... err... have you thought about getting a new pet, and keeping it in the shed from the word go? You could let it back in the house when John went to work and he's more at work than at home."

"OH DORA! How can you?" Judy demanded tearfully. "I thought you, my best friend would understand how attached I was to PD. I could never have another...none would share my life in quite the same way. I can't believe that you would suggest it."

"Calm down Judy...I only thought another kitten, or even a pet mouse, would be easier to hide from John now you know what he is capable of."

"A KITTEN! It wasn't a kitten. It was my pet German cockroach!"

A BLOKE CAN BE REAL UNLUCKY

ALEXANDER – CALLED ALEXANDER THE GREAT by his girlfriend Gwen on their first night together – had business worries, which gave him a gigantic headache. Sales in his adult shop were stable: almost nil. He had bought the business cheap, grabbed it in fact.

His shocked mother had smirked. 'The locals are all devout church-going people. I can't imagine them entering your shop for...anything. On Sundays they go the long way round to church to avoid passing the shop.'

But, mother, there's the plain brown-paper-wrapped service you know, for the needy and the curious.'

'Huh! What self-respecting wife wouldn't open a plain brown paper package addressed to her husband...I ask you!'

Alexander soon found that she was right. His 'Secret Service' mailing system did not constitute a good enough return to make it profitable. Permanently closed doors to his shop were now in sight although his mother advised him, 'perhaps you can find a buyer. There must be someone else in the world as stupid as you were, who'll buy it.'

Even Gwen, a lover of monetary esteem, who believed that being the girlfriend of a business man gave one a certain prestige, also made her position clear. 'I myself would not be seen entering such a shop, but if there's money in it dear Al – he hated being called Al – then go for it.' But now he suspected she was his ex, as he could not find a buyer for his near-bankrupt business.

These dismal thoughts possessed him as he strolled though the park on his early morning walk with Spot, his devoted 'Staffie' terrier. He hardly noticed Spot scampering around and sniffing under every bush – tail wagging vigorously in anticipation of finding a lizard or bird he could chase.

Suddenly he realised Spot was nowhere in sight. "Spot...Spot!" he called. There was no response.

He visually scanned the area. There was no sign of Spot. As he bent to look under the closest bushes, a rustle coming from somewhere ahead caused him to direct his attention to a narrow, almost completely overgrown track winding behind a grove of paper bark trees. Alexander hurried on, pushing his way through the thicket to find himself in a small clearing invisible from the road.

"Ah, there you are Spot." Relieved, Alexander strutted over to his dog who ignored him while continuing to scratch at the ground under a Melaluca tree.

"Spot – no! No smelly old bones. Thank you very much, " he commanded, at the same time stepping back as a toad hopped over his foot to disappear behind a mound of dried leaves.

When he clutched Spot's collar to drag him away, he noticed what appeared to be the corner of a box protruding from the loose soil Spot had disturbed.

"Go on Spot, scratch some more. Here, I'll help. If it's some kid's discarded lunch box and there's any food in it you can have it."

As time for opening the shop crept closer, and not wanting to cut short Spot's pleasure he decided to help. To his distaste at his dirtying hands, he finally pulled out a wooden box. He blew away the loose dirt from its lid to reveal an old-fashioned jewellery box. It was locked.

Alexander dug into his pocket for his nail clippers. Resisting the temptation to clean his nails first, he levered the stronger toenail file point between the lid and box. It sprung open.

Alexander whistled. Slender sun's rays were spiralling upwards into his face from what looked like diamonds set in several necklaces and rings. A small pile of loose cut stones lay at the bottom of the box.

Can't be real. No-one keeps good jewellery in an old box these days...bank vault's the goer. Someone's probably snatched their granny's jewellery thinking it was worth something. When they found it wasn't they got rid of it. Wait 'til Gwen hears about this. I'll be back in her good books with this lot...well...the jewellery pieces anyway. I'll keep the loose stones to taunt her with them down the track.

Alexander almost skipped as he hurried away – his failing business now furthest from his mind. Spot pranced along beside him.

Drawing out his mobile he 'phoned Gwen.

"Gwen darling I have a nice surprise for you."

"You have? I know. You've found a buyer for the shop. Good, I don't like it when you're broke. Gee, we haven't had a holiday overseas this year yet."

"Well I know this will please you. I have a beautiful ring for you, and..."

"What...a ring! You're not serious. No thank you. I wouldn't touch any supermarket ring, and that's all you can afford. Look, I'm tired of doing without. We haven't even been on that cruise you promised me either, 'cos you're broke. We're finished. You can get lost. It's over." The phone shut down with a thud.

Alexander held the purring phone for a minute as he digested Gwen's message. Slowly anger took its place. *I'll get rid of this old jewellery...get a few bob for it at the pawnbroker's, so when she decides to crawl back she'll have to take me just as I am.*

He pocketed the 'phone and looked again into the jewel box. *She's right. Who'd want a box of cheap stones and old jewellery – seen better stuff at Woolies, but, perhaps there's a reward. Granny might like to get them back. I'll try the police first.*

Now unconcerned that the shop remained unopened Alexander carried the box to the police station. Sergeant Fleming invited him into his office where he examined the contents of the box.

"Seems familiar – I recall..." He *rose and went to a cabinet where he retrieved a file. "Not everything's on computer yet." It was almost an apology.*

He opened the folder. "Yes, here it is... a report of stolen property." He spread photos on the table. Alexander had to admit it was the same jewellery.

"Stolen some time ago. We think it was by the same thief that we put away a while back over another robbery. I see here there's a reward."

Alexander beamed.

"$8,000 it says here."

Alexander stuck to his seat motionless in shock. "$8,000

reward," he gasped. His troubles were over. *When Gwen tries to crawl back I may not even consider it.* "Are you sure they're real?"

"What did you expect...phonies? Says here their total value is twenty thousand?"

Alexander's mind immediately revealed a mind-boggling fact. *If I'd sold them to Oswald the second-hand dealer I'd most likely have netted double that...all on the quiet...AND, no tax to pay either."*

The sergeant was speaking. *"Lucky you."*

"Lucky be blowed! A bloke can be real unlucky," he said in disgust.

1945

GLEN Saunders instinctively knew the long awaited news – good or bad – had arrived. Consumed with doubts and fears his gaze travelled the length of his long serge-covered legs as he stretched them out from his padded recliner, to ease the ache in his twisted leg - a 'souvenir' from World War 1. At the same time he reached sideways, and from long practice his fingers automatically closed on his unlit pipe. Its position never changed as his wife Martha left her husband's nightly relaxing area undisturbed. Its rosewood stem was smooth against his stiff fingers. He gripped it firmly between his stained teeth as he drew out a match from its box, scraping it along its side until it flared. He dipped the flame well down into the bowl of his pipe and sucked at the smoke in short puffs.

Why doesn't Martha hurry! He had seen her take a letter from the letterbox, fondle it, and wait for a few moments as if to enjoy it's very existence. Glen knew the only letter that encouraged such loving attention was from Carlos. He grew impatient. *For heavens sake Martha hurry up!*

He picked up the evening 'Telegraph' from beside his ashtray. It was full of end-of-the-war news – happy family reunions, smiling soldiers being embraced by overcome wives and mothers – children looking on bemused. In pain he cast it vigorously away from him and it fluttered towards the floor, loose pages floating air-cushioned to settle like parachutes on to the carpet. There would be no happy reunion for them. Daniel, their only child was buried beneath foreign soil; his name on a plot in New Guinea, and without Daniel the 'good news' did not have the same impact.

They had however acquired another 'son' Carlos–'adopted' when Glen befriended him when working for the American Army in Brisbane. A position that brought him into contact with Philippinos the American Navy picked up out of the sea after their ships were sunk by enemy fire. When Daniel was shipped overseas Carlos received the attention it was no longer possible to give Daniel. It was for Carlos now they worried, desperate to know whether he had success in finding his family alive in the Philippines.

His mind wandered back to Daniel, as a sweet child, as an athletic youth, as a handsome soldier. Pride mixed with sorrow which lessened with time, but never completely gone when he remembered the words of that telegram that were burned into his brain, '... killed in action'... and the dull ache increased. It had been so much worse for Martha. She stubbornly refused to believe it. He never saw her cry. Now the war was over Martha would have to accept that Daniel was never coming home.

Suddenly he became aware of Martha bustling into the lounge room. Her small hands were being wiped against her apron. She was smiling excitedly and secretly, her mouth in a tight smile. He leaned forward in expectation as she advanced towards him.

"You don't know what I've got." She then waved the letter in front of him. He could not tell her he had already guessed whom it was from. She sank into the seat beside him. "It's from Carlos. I want you to read it out loud."

He watched her expression mirror the excitement in his own eyes as she handed the letter to him. For a moment he stared at the handwriting, then at the stamp, half hoping that it was Australian, which meant Carlos was back in the country, but it was not. He lay his pipe carefully aside and with eager fingers ripped open the envelope.

Mr Saunders adjusted his glasses, cleared his throat and began reading.

"Dear Aussie Mom and Papa,

Your letter I was happy to receive. It fires my heart to think you both find time to write to me, whom you were so kind to in Australia.

You knew when we were sent back to the Philippines to help the American mop-up operations I would search for my family who I had not heard from for two years.

Sadly, I now know my father is dead. I heard that from

escapees from the war zone who came to our camp for food on our arrival in Manila. They told me he died honourably for our country. I know that would be true, as I know how great a fighter my father was. That knowledge adds pride to the sorrow of our loss.

To find information about the rest of my family I began my search as soon as I could. Firstly I look for my brother Lannie, knowing he would be with my mother and two sisters if he could, but my phone calls ended in nothing. I worried I would never find them as I was told that where we lived was now a jungle of wrecked houses and the home of ghosts.

Remember the verse in that Philippine Magazine I gave you Papa? It came back to me each time I thought of Lannie, especially those first lines. "Were you one of them my brother whom they marched under the April sun, and flogged to bleeding along the roads we knew and loved." It kept running through my mind and made me sleepless with worry.

When I had completed my duty on the first days of the mission we were part of, I was given that rare privilege, a pass, to look for my family. I still can see the concerned looks on the faces of my buddies even though they turned away to hide it as I left camp to search battered, raped, shattered Manila.

Part of my heart died when I saw the street in which I had spent my childhood – a flattened landscape – desolate, with people like scavenger ants climbing among the ruins looking for traces of their old once secure lives. I stopped strangers asking them if they knew of my family. They all shook their heads sadly and each time my heart pitched deeper in my chest, for they too were searching for someone, or something, and my answer in return to their questions was a similar regretful, 'no, sorry.'

At dusk I returned to Camp defeated and depressed, but I still clung to hope, after all it was only the first day of my search. I would next go to my Uncle's house. If he was alive and I could find him I knew he would know what happened to the rest of my family. I could not sleep, possessed by the thought that he may also be dead. When I did sleep I dreamed of searching down long streets after long streets, calling for my family but finding no-one. I woke with my face wet with tears.

The next morning, squeezed flat with misery and little sleep, my stomach churned over as we speed along the highway away from camp in a jeep I had hitched a ride in. We drove through areas where the stench was sickening; a mixture of decaying flesh – animal or human I could not guess – as well as the suffocating smell of a non-functioning sewer system and other odours I could not define, all inflamed our nostrils. Enemy equipment littered the highways, lying with their skeletal remains stabbing the sky, some blackened by exploding fire – enemy and friend dying together. The moping-up operation had hardly begun.

We swerved around people pushing carts and bundles on their backs, wearied, but determined, presumably going back to homes that may not be there. When they saw our American jeep driving alongside them they gave us the Victory sign, and yelled "Ma Boohi" (Victory) at the top of their voices. In spite of the devastation wrought by the war, they smiled at us also. True, they had lost almost all their material possessions and many were in rags, but they were alive, now free and full of hope.

Tears were again ready to splash as my eyes picked out the discarded rubble heaps which had once been the homes of friends. The beautiful sandstone school building I had once attended and the church in which I had knelt and prayed, had met the same fate – blown into piles of rubble. From the centre of one mountain of stone a cross pointed defiantly to the sky... to the heavens. Was that where my family was?

I parted with my companion at the Walled City, once a magnificent place, now scarred but still proud, and headed towards Sta Ana to my Uncle's home, but hope died when I entered his desolate street. Several people wandered aimlessly past me as I froze trying to shut out my distress as I stood before the destruction to his home. I tried to stop the growing mind-destroying thoughts of helplessness and anger, and stem the tears I knew oozed from my eyes and coursed down my face. I was not ashamed.

In bitterness I stifled the urge to shout to the heavens – to God – to scream WHY? WHY! Instead I clenched my teeth and shut my eyes to blot out the scene. I forced myself to be calm. I thought of you both in your home that you generously allowed me to share with you. I pictured the mangoes and strawberries ripening in your backyard, the peaceful river cruise to Lone Pine, the birthday party you gave me, the laughter in your home, and the friendship of Daniel. Swallowing, I pulled myself together. I must continue now to my cousin's house.

I asked many questions of the paddlers of the canoe that took me across the Pazig River, but they did not know him. From there I passed along familiar streets, and I thought of the Valeros, and the Marcelos who once lived there. My feet dragged. The poem came back to me again.

"And we would walk those roads again one April morn...fearless of death from cloudless skies." I silently recited more from that verse, and prayed the rest of my family were still alive to do so.

I hurried, looking straight ahead, past the strangers standing petrified in front of their wrecked homes. Only those who have lived through similar circumstances could know the twisted, mixed-up way I was feeling, the despair that all may be gone. As I walked I fingered the gifts in my pockets, the bracelet for Mother, the small radio for my brother, broaches for Conchita and Nena. I tried to shut out the nagging voice that said I might still have these small presents when I went back.

My cousin's house also was destroyed. I stood bewildered in front of the twisted wooden posts that once supported the entrance to a cosy well-cared-for home. They stood like unfinished crosses or sentinels beside this mound of bricks, dirt and wood – a loose mound like a new grave. I stood not moving for I do not know how long.

Then the smell of food cooking drew my attention to the Fontano's house across the street. It had been roughly rebuilt, or rather "propped up" with burnt sheets of discarded iron and patched with anything else they could find, even hessian. No-one was in sight. I walked up to a crookedly set carved solid oak door, perhaps the last remains of some rich man's mansion, most likely found lying in the street. It looked almost obscene beside the dilapidated brick wall of the house whose roof was held up with scraps of wood panels and half-burnt wooden posts. I swallowed hard and wiped my sleeve across my face and knocked.

I had not long to wait, for everyone I had met told me they waited, listening eagerly, hopefully, for a knock, which might mean someone they loved, had returned. Mrs. Fontano, a little old bent-backed lady, peered at me through a narrow opening in the door and for a moment registered a look of disbelief, before a twisted smile appeared on her cracked lips. She dragged open the shaky door and stretched out her hands, clasped mine and squealed "Gratis Dios" (Thank God) and dragged me inside.

It was dark in the house and Mrs Fontano led me to another room, held aside a ragged curtain and stood back for me to enter. I found a seated woman sewing in the half-light. My heart missed a beat then thumped as if trapped inside my chest and wanting release. I stared unbelieving – relief and joy tugging at my heart. She looked up frowning. I recognised my mother. Always small and frail she now looked old and feeble.

I was frightened she would not know me as I walked towards her. She rose slowly; Mrs Fontano helping her to stand. Then she cried with a voice betraying doubt, then hope.

"Son? Are you Carlos? It is... isn't it... Carlos... my son? Carlos!" She collapsed limp and weeping into my arms. When she quietened a little I lowered her into her chair and went on one knee before her.

"Yes mother, it is Carlos." She stroked my face and the tears flowed like a dam released to wash over her smiling lips.

"I'm not dreaming am I? It is true? Mrs Fontano, is true is it not?" The stooped Mrs Fontano stood behind my mother crying in joy for her friend. "It is true Maria. Everything will be all right now your Carlos is here. God is good."

Noise and voices mingled with sounds coming from outside the room and I turned to see Lannie and Concita enter. Lannie's face was disfigured by a long jagged scar – a long knife wound – splitting his handsome face, his smile now crooked. Conchita's face was the face of someone who had seen too much for her young years. We hugged each other, and laughed almost hysterically. We all talked at once.

I turned towards the door expecting Nena to enter. Perhaps by some miracle my father was still alive also. Heavy silence fell as everyone read my thoughts. I knew then I would never see either of them again. I would not ask how – not then anyway. To stop the visit being ruined by grief, I quickly fumbled hurriedly in my pockets and drew out the gifts. They accepted them and their wet faces kissed me together with tight hugs. They made me sit down beside them on the rough stone floor to tell them all I had seen, all I had done, and everywhere I had been.

Later that night I hitched a ride in a passing army patrol vehicle back to camp. I would apply for more leave. I had to. My homecoming, the family reunion, has not been celebrated yet. Also there will be a memorial service for my father and sister, followed by a mass of thanks-giving to God for the living. This has yet to come.

Dear Mom and Papa, with you both I grieve for our lost loved ones, but in my heart is a growing peace born of hope. The greatest pain is not knowing the truth. The fear it nurtured is gone.

Now that the war is behind us the rebuilding begins. I pray I am as strong as you both were over the loss of Daniel in New Guinea. You set me an example with your courage in your loss.

It is now almost lights out so I will finish off my writing.

Ibig (love)
from Carlos (Rivera)

....

Mr Saunders' voice broke as he finished reading. Martha's limp head was resting on her husband's shoulder and his reassuring arm tightened around her. Tears blinded her and for the first time since being advised her son had been killed, she was crying. Her body racked with the pain of realising the almost unbearable.

"Daniel is never coming back is he?" She yearned for

comfort, for denial.

"No Martha he isn't. I know you have not accepted it until now, but like Carlos we must go on with faith in the future. Carlos has his family and we have each other. The chaos of war is over."

Martha spoke between sobs. "I will try to be brave... You will help me won't you Glen? You have been so brave...you... and Carlos too."

Glen planted a light kiss on his wife's forehead wetting it with his own tears, and like Carlos he was not ashamed.

"Carlos will be as proud of you as I am. It seems Carlos, and us, have seen two different faces of the same pain, but now it's both an ending and a beginning for all of us."

He gently held his wife's face against his shoulder until her sobs died down, and continued. "I will write to Carlos and let him know that we also believe that out of all the miseries and sorrows we have had during the past years, like him we'll put it all behind us. If he can do it so can we. You will help me write the letter won't you Martha?"

He felt his wife nodding her head in agreement. She turned her tear-streaked face to his. Her lips moved and the whispered words were barely audible. "I'd like to go to New Guinea to visit Daniel's grave."

"We will dear. We will. It'll be like closing a gate on a painful past and the opening of a door to the rest of our lives together."

GODFREY SMELLS A RAT

I SMELT A RAT when Wally my rock wallaby died. They don't die like that...ever seen one that's dropped dead? I haven't and I'm eighty-one.

I smelt a dirtier 'rat' the other day when I found Cassie my canary dead in her cage. I suspected the Johnsons were behind it. They live in the unit next door and the Applebys are on the other side. So I called the cops. They weren't any help. They said I shouldn't have kept a wallaby in my town-house. If Wally wasn't dead already they would've had to charge me with cruelty or something. That's the thanks you get for looking after native species. They should be finding out what happened to those dead crows in the front yard. They're protected! Their relatives still hang around, carking like mad. I bet they know what happened, but reckon there's plenty left, so why bother.

I was on the warpath so I decided to investigate as it was now up to me. I decided to lay a trap to catch the rotten sods, because I still had Po Po the possum in the ceiling, alive and kicking. I was scared he'd be next, so I got some crowd in town to put up them sensor lights – one on the tree outside my bedroom window from where I could watch him jumping on to the roof, to go in and out of the ceiling through the broken eaves.

That night I just got to sleep when a light flashed on and straight in me eyes. I jumped up and grabbed me torch and me walking stick. I was ready for the rotten cow that was guilty. Even if it was me neighbour's cat – the Appleby's of course, not mine. Did I tell you I had cats – two in fact? I knew it wouldn't be my cats. They're too well trained, and well fed.

Then me torch shone on me possum. I swore blue murder.

The possum was on the ground with his front feet caught in a trap – in one of those string loops that they put food in the middle, and then pull the string around their legs. He looked up at me with sad eyes as if asking me for help. I raced outside and started to release him when I heard a loud voice.

"Leave him alone Godfrey. He's going into the bush today. Ha! Ha! no more sleepless nights." It was Stan Appleby standing in his doorway holding a big corn bag. I was in shock but Appleby was too late, Po Po was scrambling up the tree. Up to now I never suspected them. I knew they must have already rung the RSPCA. I had a bone to pick with him later when those outside do-gooders were gone.

When me wallaby died I was in shock and I went over and accused my other next-door neighbours, the Johnsons, of doing something ghastly to it. I didn't think the Applebys would. Of course the Johnsons said they didn't know I had a wallaby...liars! SHE came over once – the usual missus stuff – asking for a cup of sugar. Wally had jumped up on her. She had screamed blue murder and ran home. She never took the sugar.

Before lunchtime, who should turn up but the RSPCA woman. The Johnsons or the Applebys called them I reckon. This woman was in uniform and looked down her nose when she spoke. She carried on about animal rights and such. When she paused for breath I told her I'd been keeping the wallaby since it was a speck. Then she wanted to know how it died. I said I didn't know and thought that was her job.

She didn't like that none, and asked what else I had that I shouldn't have. 'Nothin,' I said, 'There's only Go Go the goanna. A big fellow, lovely he is. When I talk to him he always stares at me like he knows what I'm saying...and... there's a snake and a few turtles in me fish tanks.

She jerked her nose up in the air like as if HERS don't stink, and said, "Let the goanna loose."

I asked, "Why? He has the run of the house, even has his own bedroom, and me little back yard is his playground," but she didn't listen.

She pointed to the large hessian bag. Before she asked I told her. 'That's Wally, all ready for a grand funeral in the park across the road.' I knew the sticky-beak neighbours would be there to see it, but I hadn't got around to it yet.

She left, taking away Po Po the possum to return it to the wilds or something. I didn't see them go up on the roof where they trapped poor Po Po. They were mighty quick and quiet.

They also took the dead crows, and Wally in the bag. I gave

them dead Cassie the canary too. They said someone would come around with the authority to look over the premises for any other wildlife I might be hiding. They said I could be prosecuted. I said, 'Go ya hardest.'

When they came back they had some officials with them. That's what they called them anyway. This time they took away Go Go, the goanna. That made me see red, but I could always find another one.

I asked what had happened to Wally and the crows, what they died from. She sniffed as if disappointed and said, 'The wallaby died of old age,' which was rubbish. I only had him two years. Come to think of it, he was fully grown when I got him. She looked at me in a funny haughty way and said I could have been prosecuted for keeping protected wildlife without a licence.

I ignored that, and asked if the crows had been poisoned and if they were investigating this. She snorted, 'Crows can travel a long way.' As for me, I'm thinking it might have been the Applebys' cat killing the crows. Their cat's always chasing birds. I see theirs up the tree lots of time, not mine. Mine wouldn't hurt a fly, AND they're too well fed. I could have told her that, but I don't think she'd have listened.

As for Cassie, she said she'd died of fright, because some silly person left their pet bird outside where crows or other large birds could get at them. News to me, but I had to admit I did leave her outside on the balcony that night. I forgot about her when I started watching 'Dirty Dancing' while having me daily alcoholic 'pick-me-up.'

With all this hullabaloo going on I could see the Applebys and the Johnsons outside watching and grinning like mad. Both have been trying to make me get rid of me pets for ages. Then it hit me. It was those city slickers from the south, the Applebys, who gave me the rock wallaby. It was when they came back from their trip somewhere out bush. They knew I'd look after it they said. I should have 'smelt a rat' right then. They probably knew you had to have a licence to keep them, and didn't tell me.

I'll fix the buggers; my next pets will be a couple of cockatoos. I'm deaf.

MOVE OVER JAMES BOND: ASSIGNMENT 3

WHEN THE BALACLAVA-WEARING MAN came running from the chemist shop it was the sockless legs that betrayed the robber. His ankles became exposed as he raced away. Nardia had seen them before at very close quarters. It was the distinct 'x' shaped scar on the outside of one ankle. Miles had told her he had fallen off a cliff when he was a kid. Nardia doubted that and the thought that a previous lover had scarred him had surfaced in her mind, but why on the ankle? The recall died as she bent almost double to be concealed behind a parked car as his low cut running shoes came closer. The sound lessened as he passed. Peering out, she saw him make a long stride over the wide gutter, then disappear around the corner. Two men were chasing him but he was too fast. They returned shaking their heads with disappointment.

Nardia debated with herself as to what she should do...perhaps report her suspicions to the police who had now arrived. *No. There must be some mistake.* Her thoughts tumbled over one another. *'Maybe it wasn't him. I only had a glance. Perhaps it was only dirt that formed a similar pattern.*

Nardia shrugged and went on to finish her shopping. Still plagued with worry at the possibility of it being Miles she began to regret leaving a duplicate key to her front door hidden in an envelope in her letterbox. It was Miles' idea. He told her he was prone to losing small things like keys. It was a failing of his he had said. She thought it unusual, but as he wanted it that way she agreed to it.

When I see him I'll demand to know where he was today, whether he gets offended or not.

On arriving home laden down with her purchases, she slipped her key in the lock, then pushed the door open with her shoulder as she bundled herself and her purchases inside. Straightening up she reeled in shock. A complete stranger was sitting in her lounge chair smiling at her.

"Who...?"

"Relax, I'm Warren's friend Doug. He said to meet him here.

I was to wait outside but I found the key so I made myself comfortable. I hope you don't mind."

"How dare you! And for your information there's no Warren here. Leave before I call the police." He ignored her.

"He's Warren to me. What's he call himself now...Warren, Miles, Des? No matter, even if he's in one of his many guises, I'll know him from the 'x' on his ankle. He said he'd have something for me and I'm not leaving 'til he gets here."

He levelled his gaze at her and slowly patted his pocket.

Nardia decided that was a hint he had a gun and backed away.

"Don't worry lady. I won't be staying once your Miles gets here. Look lady, I've got no beef with you, but I don't want you to cause any trouble for us. Look, make some coffee and in no time we'll be gone." She had a strong urge to object, but decided it might be safer not to. She turned towards the kitchen and he rose to follow her, but before she could move forward he asked.

"Where'd you meet Warren/Miles?"

"College."

"Ah...selling drugs to the students...smart move."

"Drugs! Never!"

"I see he's kept it from you. Smooth lad is our Warren. Safe as houses cottoning on to someone clean like you, but your Miles is into drugs, and I'm here to collect what he owes his supplier.'

The sound of the front door opening made them both turn. In the doorway stood Miles. He first greeted the visitor. "G'day mate...knew you'd be here." He then walked over to Nardia and quickly kissed her on the cheek. She was shocked at his audacity. Before she could make a quick retort, he was walking towards their bedroom. Nardia was about to follow him but he waved her back. She remained standing, nervous and frightened.

He reappeared, weighted down by his belongings. Doug relieved him of his suitcase, and the two men prepared to leave. The stranger reached the door first, while Miles slipped an arm around Nardia who squirmed away, fearful they would take her with them, but he dropped his arm and smiled his boyish grin.

"It was nice Nardia...never forget you. Maybe we can get

together again when I'm in town."

"If you ever come within a kilometre of me I'll call the police and tell them you're a drug dealer."

He laughed. It was a laugh Nardia had loved for its happy sound. "And what will you tell them my sweet? You have no proof I have anything to do with drugs so who would believe you? No one knows I've been staying here with you so I can say I've never met you. 'Bye sweetheart…till next time I see you." He followed Doug out and she bolted the door behind them.

Shaking, she quickly went to the window to be sure they had actually left. Miles saw her. He smiled and waved. In his hand were the keys of a car. He did not own one and she had not seen any car out front when she had returned home, but now there was one.

Worried she might find traces of drugs Nardia checked the house, but the only reminder of Miles was a statue he had brought her on her birthday. It was positioned on the top of the television set. 'That's going out tomorrow,' she decided.

What if he comes back? She checked to make sure all windows and access doors were securely locked. Knowing Miles still had a key she pushed the heaviest lounge chair against the front door.

She sank down into the closest chair knowing that any story she told would have a ring of a disgruntled thrown-away lover to it. *What can I do? I know I've been tricked but what can I do? I have to do something, but what?* She knew she would firstly have to prove he actually existed. He always said he was too busy studying when she wanted him to go with her to meet her friends. Now she realised it was part of his hide and seek games.

That night she slept spasmodically. Lying awake at 6am she decided she could not remain alone and scared. *There's no way I'm going to leave the place today, but I need advice and company.* She immediately notified her workplace that she would not be in that day, then called her girlfriend Meta. On hearing Nardia's urgent request, Meta immediately promised to be there as soon as she could.

Half an hour later, seated together on the lounge, Meta was comforting Nardia as she related the whole series of events. "He told me his ex-wife was after him for half his bank account and their house, so he had to keep out of sight as she wasn't entitled to any of it and was hassling him with a solicitor. He made me promise I wouldn't tell anyone he was living with me. I believed him. How dumb can you be?"

"We all make mistakes Nardia, but drugs? That's bad. You could have been involved. You're lucky he left."

"But he might come back," was the nervous response.

"True, so you must tell the police. They'll keep an eye on the place I'm sure." Meta rose. "I'll make us a nice cup of tea."

As she passed the TV she remarked. "What happened to that photo you had on the small table...the one of you with your favourite uncle?"

"I don't know. Perhaps I put it somewhere else. I can't remember."

"You looked lovely in that photo. Maybe Miles took it for a keepsake."

This made Nardia smile. "That's the joke of the week. He didn't like me. He used me."

"So we have to make sure he doesn't come back. You must tell the police."

Nardia agreed, knowing she had no choice if she were to protect herself from him in the future.

....

At the Drug Squad's headquarters the Chief Executive Officer, Mr Grant Stand, called in Ernest Moneylove, worshipper and devotee of that famous film undercover spy, James Bond, into his office.

"We've had a report that a drug dealer we're looking for, a Desmond Miles Warren has finally been traced. He's an expert in disguise, which has made him impossible to catch so far. He's been staying with a Nardia Barlow. This is a photo of her."

Ernest studied it carefully and handed it back. *She's quite a James Bond beauty.*

His boss continued. "She thinks he may come back again,

though I think it's mighty unlikely, at least for a while. But I'm assigning you to watch her house anyway. If he comes back you can call on the police back-up to arrest him. If you succeed it will be a 'feather in your cap,' so to speak."

"Thank you sir," was Ernest's enthusiastic response while straightening up and pushing out his flat chest. *It's not a James Bond type of job, except for the beautiful girl involved, but it's on the way up so start moving over James.*

His boss continued. "The house was checked and some white power was found inside a rather large carved statue he had given Nardia. It had been hollowed out and stuffed with a large number of $100 notes. We believe he'll come back to collect it, though I'm sure he'll lie low for a few weeks at least. He wouldn't be stupid enough to show up in the daylight, but we have to be ready. I know it's a menial job but you are the one best suited for it."

James Bond never turned down a job. At least I won't have that sneaky undermining Smithy taking the credit for something I've achieved. He's on some other job. He narrowed his eyes and jutted out his chin as he has seen James Bond do in his films. "Thank you sir."

"You are to cruise past her home several times a day, and sit in the car near the big tree from ten to midnight. Grab anyone – you will have backup – who comes within proximity of the house and is acting even slightly suspiciously. Success in this job will help you up the ladder, so DON'T blow it this time."

"I won't sir."

Several days later when the sun had set and it was becoming too dark to continue reading, Ernest put down his book of spy stories. He was beginning to feel hunger twisting his empty stomach into a knot.

About to start the car engine he saw the upper part of a man's body blacking out the side window. He was elderly with a white beard. He knocked on the window nearest to Ernest, who lowered it.

He talked slowly and coughed almost constantly as he spoke. "Sorry to trouble you mister." He pointed to Nardia's house. "Is that No. 3? My sight's bad and I can't read numbers, especially as it's got so dark. I'm Nardia's uncle and I have a present I promised her. It's a lovely framed photo of both of us." He ripped the paper from the packet he was holding, exposing a framed photo. He held it up for Ernest who switched on the overhead light. "You see, that's Nardia and that's me."

Ernest nodded. He noted the likeness of the man to the one in the photo with Nardia. He had no doubts they were the same.

"She's my favourite niece. I'll just go in and give it to her. She's going to love it."

"I suppose she would." Moneylove agreed. The man waddled off and Ernest watched him reach the front door.

Ernest checked his watch, and then drove himself to a McDonald's Take Away food outlet.

....

"Hello Nardia."

Nardia swung around, puzzled. The door had been locked. The man in front of her would pass for her uncle but she recognised the voice. It was Miles. She thought of screaming but knew that if he became violent it would be too late for the guard to reach her in time, so she decided to try to bluff him.

"I can see how you fooled the police, but I'm going to scream if you don't get out." With her heart pounding she willed it to be a success.

"That guard of yours won't hear you. He's gone for his dinner. Always does at this time every night. All I want is the statue and you won't hear from me again." She knew she had failed.

Suddenly the door flung open and in rushed two policemen with guns ready to fire. A man wearing a drug squad badge whom Marcia did not recognise accompanied them.

Miles did not move as they arrested him. As they were marching him to the door he turned back to Nardia. "Nice knowing you sweetheart. 'Bye till next time." Before she could say 'dream on,' they had gone.

When Ernest returned holding a large hamburger, he was

astounded to see 'pushy' Smithy, the fellow drug officer determined to rise to the top with the least effort and at Ernest's expense, marching out of the property with two policemen who were holding on to the man he believed was Nardia' uncle.

When told the man was the drug courier they were after, Ernest thought, 'Fancy it being her uncle. I thought the dealer would be much younger. Even James Bond would have had difficulty with this one.'

Smithy, with a satisfied grin on his face added. "The Boss thought I should check on how you were doing. Lucky I did. Nardia won't be troubled with this bloke again after we've dealt with him."

As they arrived at the police van Smithy turned back to Ernest. "This will go good on my record, shame you missed out…again."

Moneylove wanted to kick him in the shins, but instead he comforted himself. *James Bond had his set backs too, but he made up for it on his next assignment, and that's what I'll be doing. Just you wait Smithy.*

HIS OWN MAN

"I'D forget him if I were you Anita. He's weird." Claudia would feel guilty if she did not voice her opinion to her older sister.

"You really think that don't you Claudia, but if you knew him you'd think differently."

"Perhaps, but I doubt it. His hair is long and looks dirty. His clothes are only clean because you wash them for him. Anyone who wears odd coloured and usually dirty socks, and keeps his little finger nails an inch or more long, which he guards zealously, is more than a little strange, in my opinion."

Anita laughed. "That's my big sister talking. Those are things I like about Ruckus. There's much more to him than you know. For instance, he had his name changed legally, because he's his own individual, not bent down under the yolk of convention. He's his own man. As for long nails, each one is a pointer to hypocrisy of large corporate so-called civilisation . . . cool hey?"

"Only a young Uni student like you would connect to that outlook, but my advice, which I know you won't take, is drop him, and sooner the better."

"Never, he's the most exciting man I know. He believes in expressing his fundamental basic right to freedom of expression in whatever way he chooses. One way is by lighting a cigarette in a prohibited areas daring people to tell him to stop. He's a big man so they usually ignore him.

"Be warned Anita. He's asking for trouble. But I must go or *I'll be late for work....bye.*"

Claudia was too busy to think about Anita's crush on Ruckus over the next few weeks, but when she read in the newspaper that Ruckus was arrested and charged with assaulting someone in a supermarket she rang Anita immediately.

"Sorry Claudia. I've been going to ring you. Ruckus has been sentenced to a whole month in jail. I can't wait until I visit him in prison. I just can't wait." Anita expressed so much devotion to Ruckus, Claudia groaned inwardly.

"Oh Anita, I hope you know what you're doing. I think now is a good time for you to back off."

"It wasn't his fault. People are always picking on him and he has to defend himself. I'll never let him down. I'll stay by him forever, no matter what." Claudia despaired of changing Anita's mind and remained silent.

Several days later Claudia was surprised when she found a distressed Anita waiting for her when she returned from work.

Once inside, with both seated comfortably and holding a steaming cup of freshly made coffee, Anita could not wait any longer to explain.

"Oh Claudia I should have listened to you and given Ruckus a wide berth, but all I could see was an individual brave enough to be his own person and not be dictated to by money or by our restricting society, but now I find he's..." Anita let out a sob.

"He's what? What happened?"

"He's disgusting . . . uncouth. I saw him today for the first time since his arrest. He wasn't at all interested in ME. He didn't seem to care whether I was there or not, and I was so happy to see him. All he did was bemoan the loss of that long pointed fingernail. That's what the fight in the supermarket was about. Apparently a man swerved his trolley into Ruckus. He quickly pushed it away, but ended up breaking off one of his long fingernails. That's when he downed the bloke."

"Why was that such a bad thing...about the finger nail, I mean. He can always grow it again...heaven forbid."

"It was for Ruckus. He told me it was a tragedy, as it would upset his daily routine. He believes strongly in order...despises leaders who do nothing to bring order back into today's chaotic world. He always keeps strictly to a set routine and I always admired him for it."

Claudia restrained from interrupting, thinking that perhaps odd dirty socks were part of his new world order.

Anita continued. "Now his routine is upset. He was very upset about it. He said that at exactly the same time each day without fail he used his nails to clean out his ears...now his timing's ruined. That's creepy. I walked out. If it's one thing I can't stand it's weird people."

Claudia gave a sigh, gently patting Anita's hand in sympathy.

LOVE BOUNCES

MARIO MACINO LOOKED THROUGH THE WINDOW beside his office desk and waited. It was 9.15am. The blonde beauty would be passing along the street below his window any minute now. *There she is.* From the distance he scanned her face, her form. He knew when she changed her mode of dress and which hairstyle she favoured. His favourites were, when her shoulder-length hair was bounced around by the breeze, allowing it to form a halo around her face, and when her mini skirts showed most of her shapely legs. His eyes always travelled down her body, and he was almost overcome with desire for her when her tight dress pulled across her rear as she mounted the stairs to the gym across the street, where she worked.

He sucked in his breath, pulling in the soft roundness of his stomach. He believed he was in good physical shape for one on the eve of retirement. He wished he could find a way to spend it with the blonde he watched every day. That she was the age of some of his junior staff did not concern him. He told himself he still had many good years and considered himself more than a match for any young, impulsive, ignorant young fellow. 'Experience counts,' he thought, 'and money.'

This particular Monday however was different. He felt both sad and pleased. Margie had walked out on him. Although it had been coming for some time he did not want to face the future alone. *She'll be sorry.* His last girlfriend got boring so he was now free. Perhaps he could interest the blonde. He decided it was time to take the first step.

At his lunch break he walked across to the gym. At the counter was seated the blonde. He sucked in his breath as she leaned forward, reaching for her receipt book, her low cut front showing more than he had hoped to see so soon. "Can I help you sir?" she enquired.

"Oh... oh yes. I would like to join."

"Certainly sir." Her voice was music to his ears. "I'm Jenny, and you are?"

"Mario Macino...Mario if you like." He held his breath. She was about to say his name as her eyes met his.

"Well Mario, welcome. Now tell me what you want to achieve and I'll design an exercising plan to suit your needs."

Mario stared at Jenny's full scarlet painted lips. His mind conjured up visions of pressing them with his own while their bodies clung together, with Jenny breathless with rapture when they parted.

"Sir? sir!"

"Oh…oh yes. Perhaps you can work out something for me." He wanted to keep her talking. The sexy vision must not vanish, not yet. Mario felt he was in love again – his many past 'loves' now almost forgotten, or dismissed as mistakes. 'This time it will be permanent,' he told himself for the countless time.

From each Monday onwards his lunch break was spent moving half-heartedly through his exercise routine while keeping watch on Jenny through his half-closed lids. He did not want to stare openly. She may think he was some sort of pervert, but the pressure she used when she helped him to position his arms or body correctly, was to Mario a 'come-on'.

Weeks passed, during which he made himself somewhat helpful at the gym and chatted to Jenny whenever he could. She became friendlier. He found out she lived with her widowed mother…no complications there. She told him she wanted to travel, especially to New Zealand. That was the hint he wanted. He was ready to make his move. He collected New Zealand travel brochures. He would suggest she come with him, all expenses paid. Or perhaps, if he bought the tickets – offered her one – she would not refuse. *Unmarried couples are common on trips these days.*

The following Monday, with the purchased tickets warming in his shirt pocket he arrived early at the gym. He planned to tell her about the proposed trip before she arrived and became busy – convinced that as she only worked on a part-time basis she would be thrilled and agree immediately. He went over in his mind what he would say. *I mustn't sound pushy. I'll make out it's a gift for her help. I'll sneak up on the subject – thank her for her helpful assistance and advice with my losing weight efforts…good idea.*

As he waited, and no Jenny arrived he became impatient. *Where is the girl?* He stayed seated, forgetting everything except

Move Over James Bond

Jenny.

He attracted the attention of another assistant. "Can I help Mario?"

"...err...I wanted to ask Jenny something...about my programme of course. Will she be in today?"

The assistant smiled. "Didn't you know? She got married on Saturday. She's on her honeymoon...lucky girl."

Mario's face drained. *How dare she lead me on like that – not tell me.* "I didn't know," he muttered. "She never wore any rings."

"It's not allowed 'cause of some of the machinery she handles...might get caught you know. Now, what is it you wanted to ask before your workout? Perhaps I can help."

"I don't feel up to exercising today. I'll give it a miss."

The puzzled assistant watched Mario as he almost stumbled in his hurried escape down the stairs. *All that money on the tickets! She encouraged me – let me think she was interested in me and then goes off and marries someone – some uncouth bloke her own age I bet. She'll be sorry. I could have given her much more than some half-baked kid.*

The days passed and Mario slowly convinced himself that he had had a lucky escape. *When she returns and tells me the marriage didn't work, I'll tell her she brought it on herself.* He sighed. *Or perhaps I'll be kind – be ready to comfort the poor girl. She'll be grateful.*

The following Monday, from force of habit, Mario looked out the window half expecting Jenny to reappear, very unhappy, having cut ties with her 'useless' husband. As his eyes drifted across the people walking below he suddenly gasped. *"Jenny?"* No, this woman seemed taller. Her face was turned away but the hair and the walk was Jenny's. There was however something different. She walked slower, with shoulders slightly stooped, due Mario decided to her disappointment in her new mate.

At his lunch break he clamoured down to the gym, ready to give Jenny his shoulder to cry on, plus all the trappings of sympathy he could muster. When he entered the gym the blonde head was bent, face down over the papers on her desk. "Jenny." He blurted out. The head lifted and Jenny's eyes looked at him, but it was not Jenny. This woman was much older.

"Sorry, Jenny's extended her honeymoon. Mitchell has been offered a well-paying job over there so they are checking it out.

Can I help?" She smiled...Jenny's mouth...Jenny's smile, but a face with wrinkles around her eyes and lips.

"Don't look so surprised. I'm Jenny's mother, Estelle. I'm filling in for Jenny 'til she comes home from New Zealand. I'd love to go there myself. Maybe I will one day."

He remembered the tickets in his pocket. Mario smiled. Everything about Estelle was a duplicate of Jenny except for the obvious age difference in figure and face. *Maybe I should ask her. I could always close my eyes and pretend it was Jenny. Estelle is sure to want to see Jenny over there, and of course I'd be with her. It's a way to get close to Jenny and be there when that husband of hers turns out to be a big mistake on her part.*

"I'm pleased to meet you Estelle. Could we go over my routine together?"

In due course and close to the departure date, Mario, now on friendly terms with Estelle, asked her to lunch at the local restaurant. She gladly accepted.

After several wines, with Mario giving Estelle his unfailing attention, he told her in the saddest tone he could muster, of his disappointment about his almost ex-wife, and how he had tickets to take her to New Zealand but now they would be wasted.

"It's a shame to let the tickets go to waste. Perhaps I could persuade you to come along with me." He used the hopefully expectant look he kept for such occasions.

"I'd love to, now that we're such good friends," Estelle replied, looking up at him and smiling happily. From that moment he treated her like some precious ornament fearful she may change her mind and he would not see Jenny and bring her home as he planned.

The day of departure arrived. Estelle told him she would meet him at the airport as she had last minute items to attend to. Mario was a little nervous wondering if his great plan had come unstuck.

Finally she arrived. Mario was shocked to see her holding a toddler in her arms.

"What?" he spluttered.

Estelle turned the baby to face Mario. "Meet Lindy, she's Jenny and Mitchell's baby. They missed her so much they asked me to bring her over to them seeing I've got the opportunity now, thanks to you. I can't thank you enough. Isn't she gorgeous? We're all going to have a wonderful time.

Mario, don't walk so fast. I can't keep up."

LOVE IS LIKE THE MEASLES

'LOVE IS LIKE THE MEASLES – more dangerous when it comes late in life,' goes the old adage. But that's wrong. It's like bloody ringworm. It gets you in a tight circle, itches, and although you treat it nice, it can still irritate you. Okay! You're right. When you get past all that, it can be bloody beautiful. But I decided it wasn't worth it, so I swore off it. Now the family says I've turned into a grumpy old biddy, and they've stopped comin' over. That made me change me will. They'll get nothin'.

Anyway I've got a new friend, Bernie from next door. He's lots younger. When I get mean to him, **he** still comes over.

One afternoon on me walk down the creek I fell. I couldn't get up. I shouted. It got dark and cold. I thought 'I'm going to die'. I was moaning when Bernie found me.

Later, when I opened me eyes, I found I was in me own bed. Me two kids were smiling down at me.

"You had a slight stroke Mum but you'll be okay."

They were so happy I wasn't going to cark it, right then I made up me mind. I shouted. 'Get me solicitor. I want to change me will.'

Then Bernie leaned over me. His paws pressed me chest as he licked me face.

Well I guess love ain't like ringworm, it **is** like the measles! Once the flush is gone; it still stays in the system.

THE SECOND ADAM

NEWINA woke to the sound of the whirling of a large motor rising to a high pitch, and then dropping back down to a throb. Her eyes flicked open. A bright light from outside flooded the bedroom. Curious, she scrambled out of bed to look out of the open window, but she was almost blinded by the incoming glare. All she could discern was what appeared to be a large round metal disk hovering over the lawn. Its single light was beaming directly towards her. *A U.F.O? No, only deranged people believe in flying saucers. It must be some prank by that rough crowd next door.*

She swung around to what seemed to be an intake of breath, combined with a shuffling sound coming from behind. She was fearful she would sight an intruder, but she was momentarily blinded by the sudden change from light to dark. She groped for the bedside lamp. In her effort, one foot hooked the leg of the bed. She fell. A pain stabbed the side of her head as she crashed to the floor. She cried out as blackness swallowed her and she knew no more.

Newina awoke at the ringing of her alarm clock. It was 6.30 am. She found herself lying comfortably beneath the blankets on her bed. She shuddered when she recalled the night's episode. *The window was open, now it's closed. There was a light outside. I fell over. I was on the floor. Now I'm in bed.* She felt her head but there was no tenderness. *Heavens, I hope I never have a nightmare like that again.*

By the time she left for work at Dr Whimsy's generic engineering research laboratory, the memory was fading.

During the next few months Newina experienced sudden mood swings that she could not control, nor understand. Between bouts she felt normal, except her food intake increased and weight gain followed. A fellow worker remarked on her weight gain. "I hate to say this Newina, but your extra weight is making you hard to work with. I had a weight gain once and I took tablets only prescribed by a doctor. I suggest you do the same."

"I know I've been hard to work with lately, and I've been going to do something about it but thought it might right itself on its own. If you give me his name I'll go and see him."

"Okay. I have it here." She drew out a card from her bag and handed it to Newina.

"Thanks. I'll make an appointment now."

That evening, seated in the doctor's surgery she explained why she was there. "I've only come for slimming tablets. I've gained so much weight it's embarrassing."

"Have you any other symptoms?" he asked as he prepared to take her blood pressure.

Newina hesitated. "Well I've had some mood swings and leg pains."

"I think you should have a thorough check-over."

"I'm very fit otherwise."

Nevertheless, after more pressure from the doctor, she submitted to a thorough examination. She expected him to automatically write out a prescription for the tablets she wanted, but instead, she listened in horrified silence to his diagnosis.

"You have another three months to go in your pregnancy and will need regular check-ups."

"What! Pregnant! You're wrong doctor. It's not possible. Since my divorce there has been no one. There must be something else, excess fluid perhaps or a tumour. Why I had a friend once...."

The doctor cut her off. "My examination clearly denotes pregnancy. However I'm somewhat puzzled. The foetus is long and seems to be in an unusual position with an extra attachment I seem to feel, and the heartbeat has a rhythm I haven't heard before. I'd like to carry out a scan. If there is anything dangerous to you or the child it is better to find out now."

Nausea consumed Newina and the blood drained from her face as she recalled her 'nightmare'. The time element would fit. She had been certain someone was in her flat that night. *Who?* She remembered the flying saucer shaped object she perceived outside. *Was it a U.F.O? Has some slimy green man from Mars impregnated me?* She could not block out the repulsive thought. *I've read such stories. What if they're true? If they are than what will happen to the baby? Would they take it away for experimental purposes? Would I* become the centre of attention as the mother of an odd infant some would call a freak?

"Are you all right?" The doctor's voice brought her back to reality. "Here, take this before you collapse on me." The doctor handed her a glass of water and a tablet. "Obviously I've given you a shock, but perhaps there's been a time that seems vague... too much alcohol intake maybe. There can also be reasons why a young woman blocks out the memory of an intimate contact. Sometimes it's through guilt."

She swallowed the tablet and drank the water. "What kind of unusual shape?" she forced herself to ask.

"Just different and perhaps a little advanced in its development. I'm sure a scan will prove everything's normal."

Normal? Normal? What if it's a freak? Hell, I must get control of myself. I'm being absurd. She rose. "I'll ring and make an appointment later in the week."

"Don't leave it too long. Goodnight."

"Goodbye," muttered Newina as she hurried out to her car.

Newina began to sleep less and eat erratically, from oversized meals to none at all. She resorted to wearing loose-fitting tops and baggy slacks. She became edgy and at times clumsy. "Hell!" she exclaimed when she dropped a phial while Professor Whimsy was working on some new tests. He shouted at her. "Get out. Go and do bookwork or something."

Dr Foster, Dr. Whimsy's assistant, took her arm and guided her into his office. "Newina, you're shaking. Relax and tell me what's being going on with you over the last few months. What's wrong? You know I'd do anything for you. You only have to ask."

"Thanks, but it's just that I'm haven't been feeling well, a virus or something."

Dr Foster ignored the inference. "Is it your ex-husband Rodney? Has he been harassing you again?"

Is Rodney the intruder? She had not considered this aspect before as he was now nothing to her and she rarely gave him a thought. Newina's mind skipped back to when Rodney disappeared with all their savings, leaving behind a mountain of bills. She was still struggling to survive. She longed to own her own home as they had once planned, but she would need $80,000 to start looking and that was nothing more than a pipe dream.

Newina suddenly recalled he had a duplicate key for the front door and could still have it. She also knew that if it were Rodney he would be looking for money. She had little in the flat and would have noticed if that had been missing. She felt both angry at that possibility but also strangely relieved. *Even he would be preferable as a father, rather than some creepy unknown monster.*

"Newina, are you with me?" She slowly nodded. "Good. It's obvious that you need rest and attention for this... er... virus, so I want you to take, say, a few months off. " His eyes rested for a moment on her shape. "You've sick leave entitlement and some accrued leave due, so that will be no problem."

Newina was aware of Lionel's deep feelings for her and longed to confide in him, but she dared not. *He'll think I'm mental.* "I don't need months. A few weeks perhaps." *Surely in that time I'll have worked out what to do next.*

"You need more than a few weeks." He once again glanced at her enlarged body. When Newina said nothing, he added, "As second in charge I could insist you take extended leave of three months but let's agree to six weeks at least."

"Well, all right, six weeks." Newina desperately wanted to escape his scrutiny. Stirred by his obvious concern, she felt she might blurt out something she might regret later.

"I'll arrange the paper work. You can leave as soon as you're ready. But if you decide you want to get right away from everything for a while Dr Whimsy has often mentioned some resort he favours."

Newina wished she <u>could</u> go and hide somewhere <u>forever</u>, but she realised it was pointless using up precious money she needed for other items. "No thanks. I'll be able to fill in the time quite well."

"I'm sure you can, but I'll ring you now and again to see if you're okay."

"Thanks Lionel. That'd be good." She struggled to smile.

Newina bade her farewells and left.

During the next two days Newina sank into the depth of fear and depression. On the third morning, while pacing around her flat she noticed an envelope had been slipped under her door. She picked it up. *It's Lionel's handwriting. Perhaps he wants me back.* She ripped open the envelope in a frenzy of anticipation and read.

'Dear Newina,

First, I hope you're enjoying your break, but I am writing mainly to ask if you'd like to take advantage of the enclosed. I would have handed it to you personally, but am on overtime – too late to call in on my way home. The truth is, Professor Whimsy is worried about you too, and said his daughter Fiona has accepted a job overseas so can't go to Ferndale Resort for a holiday. It's somewhere near Alice Springs, and as it's too late to get a refund he thought you might like to accept a six-week stay at the resort, all-inclusive, in her place. I think he wants you back safe and well as soon as possible and this would hurry things along.

The name on the bus ticket can't be changed so you'll have to be Fiona Whimsy until you get there. He said to tell you he doesn't want any reimbursement as he considers this a good way to express his appreciation for the extra work you put in when I was ill. I also think he's sorry he shouted at you. Please accept, and after a few days there, I know you'll ring me to say you're having a wonderful time and feel on top of the world.

Bye, Lionel.

P.S. We all miss you, especially <u>me</u>. The lab isn't the same without you.'

Newina was in two minds about the offer. *I don't like accepting favours especially from my boss. Maybe he is sorry but there are others more worthy of it than me. It's a bit strange, but it would mean less time to mope about in my flat doing nothing but worry.*

She rang and spoke to Lionel. Dr Whimsy he said was too busy to talk. He seemed to be extremely excited she had accepted the offer, but reminded her that she must leave that afternoon.

With speed she packed more clothes than she believed she would need, then hired a taxi to take her to the bus depot. Fifteen minutes later, comfortably seated, Newina began to feel a sense of excitement as the bus pulled out into the traffic. Her holiday had begun.

Time passed slowly and Newina became bored. After consuming the refreshments provided she closed her eyes and drifted into a sleep-like condition. A man's voice eventually brought her out of it. Opening her eyes she was surprised to find it was dark outside and the bus was empty of other passengers. *Must be the end of the line.* She turned towards the voice. Two men were standing in the aisle looking down at her.

One spoke. "Fiona Whimsy is booked to go on to Ferndale Resort. I've come to pick her up."

The uniformed man whom she vaguely recalled was the driver, tugged at her sleeve, urging her to rise. 'Come along, Miss Whimsy. I hate disturbing you but we don't want you to miss your connection." As she rose he moved aside to allow her to pass.

Newina stepped down on to a grass verge made visible by the beams from the vehicle's headlights. She waited while the other man collected her luggage and loaded it into the back of a stationary 4WD mini-van parked behind the bus. It had 'Fernvale Retreat' painted on its side.

The man opened the rear door and assisted her to mount its high step. Newina noticed a very young girl already inside. She was asleep, and obviously pregnant. Shortly after settling in and listening to the drone of the motor she became drowsy, and caught snatches of sleep.

Strong arms encircling her body and almost lifting her out of the van jerked her to full awareness. "What's happening? Who are you?"

"I am Elam."

"Elam?"

"A strange name yes. It's back-to-front."

"I don't understand, and you can take your arms away. I can get out myself."

"Of course. You are at the resort now. I will escort you to your room. Tonight we will bring your dinner to you. Tomorrow you can mix with our other guests."

Newina welcomed the thought of stretching out on a comfortable bed after sitting for so long. She glanced around but the other girl was nowhere to be seen.

Elam led her through the ornate entrance of the high-class resort and into a foyer filled with hand-carved maple furniture. Perfume peppered the air from the fresh flowers resting in exquisitely moulded crystal vases on tables and in alcoves. *I'm going to love it here.*

At her room Elam swung open the door for Newina to enter. He followed closely with her luggage and placed it on several racks.

"The waiter will bring your dinner in thirty minutes." Then Elam was gone.

Newina unzipped her case, took out her night attire and personal items and enjoyed a leisurely shower.

Cool and refreshed she made herself comfortable on the low soft-cushioned settee. *This is nice. Fiona Whimsy sure knows how to pick the best.*

She turned her head at the sound of a knock. 'Come in.'

A young waiter entered and placed a tray on the table. "I'm Revol... welcome to Ferndale."

"Thanks. You also have an unusual name."

"Not when you look back at it. Should you require anything further please press the button above the desk." Before she could ask him to explain further, he had left, closing the door silently behind him.

The following morning Newina found her way to the dining room where Revol guided her to the table at which the teenage girl from the van was seated.

She smiled widely at Newina. "My name's Una."

"I'm Newina. We came in the same van, but you were fast asleep."

"How long are you going to be here?"

"Six weeks."

"I'm staying 'til I have the baby. They've a doctor over in one of those other buildings. It's the only medical centre for miles around. I don't know how mother knew of this place way out here in the sticks. It's somewhere between Alice Springs and Darwin she said. Mum made all the arrangements when I told her I was sick of staying with friends so Dad wouldn't find out. They'll find a good home for it. It's all hush hush you know. I don't want to face my friends or my father with a baby in tow. Besides, I have to finish my uni course."

"What about the baby's father?"

"Don't know who it is. I was too out of it. It was a wild party."

Newina's stay passed quickly, during which she kept her fears under control and her tears at bay. She became sad at the thought of leaving and facing reality again, and expressed her reluctance to Una.

"Please, please, Newina, stay longer." Una begged. "I'll miss you."

"Sorry, but I'm a bit low in funds so I'll have to be off, although I'd like to stay until your baby is born. I'd love to see him... or her."

"I don't think you will. The doctor is arranging an immediate adoption, and mother thinks it's best not to see the child at all and that suits me. Look, here's breakfast."

Shortly after, when back in her room, Elam entered and seated himself beside Newina.

"I hear you would like to stay longer. We would be pleased to have you."

"I'm sorry, I can't."

"Newina, I do not want to upset you, but would you like to tell me your plans? I realise you are alone. We have helped others. Perhaps we can assist you also. If you don't want to discuss your pregnancy we will forget this conversation."

Newina stared at Elam who looked the essence of compassion, and dark despair washed over her, threatening to drown her in it as she spoke. "I don't know what to do, and I don't have much time left to decide one way or the other. I want to keep the child, but that means I'll have some serious reorganising and relocating to do. I just don't know where to start."

"May I suggest that you remain here until the baby is born and then decide? You may even want to consider adoption."

"I'd have to get more time off, but because of my financial position…"

"If it is mainly worry about funds, and all working people without doting parents like Una have money worries, I will make an offer. We are short in the kitchen, so if you are willing to help, your pay will cover everything. Does that appeal to you?"

The offer seemed attractive. "I would like to but I will have to get more time off work."

"That will be no problem. If you write out a note for your employer, and one to your landlord, telling them you are too sick to return yet and will pay the rent on your return, I will send them off for you."

"Thanks."

A burden seemed to have been lifted from Newina's shoulders, at least for the time being.

When she met up with Una at afternoon tea Una was delighted. "I'm so pleased Newina. We've been having such a good time together."

Perhaps I should follow Una's lead and have the baby adopted out straight away, but could I? No! Anyway I have weeks in which to make the final decision, but for now I'm not going to dwell on it.

Newina commenced her kitchen duties, which gave her ample time to spend happily with Una, exploring the extensive facilities of the resort. Una was close to motherhood, when she announced, "The doctor wants to see me tomorrow. I think the baby's coming early, which is okay by me. The sooner the better."

Newina waited patiently for Una at lunch the following day, but she did not appear. Worried, she asked Elam, "Is Una all right?"

"I believe the doctor has confined her to bed."

"Can I see her?"

"Tomorrow perhaps. I will ask."

Newina waited anxiously the rest of the day for news and was becoming edgy, especially as she could not see Elam anywhere. The following morning Elam came to her room. "Una sent you this note."

Newina eagerly unfolded it and read.

'To my friend Newina,

The good news is that it's all over and I've got my figure almost back. The doctor tells me I had a daughter but I didn't see her. Mother knows best.

When they told me there was a car going to the coast and there wouldn't be another for a week or more, I had a big rush to be on it. Sorry I couldn't say goodbye in person. Thanks for being my friend, but now I can't get home quick enough.

Good luck.... Una.'

Newina was deeply disappointed.

Before what she believed was the due date for the birth, Newina reached the final stages of pregnancy. In panic and pain she called for Elam. He immediately drove her to the infirmary,

Newina was amazed to discover a sophisticated miniature hospital located within high windowless walls adjoining a chemist shop front. The nurse called the doctor and held her still while she was being given a needle. She tried to protest – to tell them she wanted to be conscious during the birth but it was to no avail. She fought against the drug's effect but finally she sank into a sea of non-awareness.

Newina's senses returned suddenly. It may have been due to her determination to witness the birth, or the wailing of an infant. She fought for clear focus at the nurse who was holding up an infant. In shock and disbelief she viewed the small body. The baby's skin was thick and grey. The little hands had long curved nails. The little face was a caricature of a lizard-human with large round eyes, heavy lids, a long nose, wide mouth and a protrusion like a tail, an inch or so long showing at the end of the spine. She realised that it was her child – her son.

Possessed with the conviction that she had given birth to some alien monster's child her screams echoed around the walls of the room. She felt the prick of a needle in her upper arm and after a few seconds she knew no more.

When she finally came back to consciousness she was ready

to ask for her baby, but hesitated when she saw two strangely dressed figures standing at the end of her bed. Large caps shaded their faces. They wore gloves, and although dressed in long coats their bodies seemed to be out of shape somehow, but she could not define it exactly. She tried to shout for the nurse, but it emerged as merely a moan.

"Newina, do not be alarmed. We are your friends," one said in an accent Newina could not recognise.

"Where's the doctor? I want to talk to him." Her voice was weak and strained.

"He will come later. Relax Newina. All we need to know is whether you plan to take your child with you when you leave?"

Tears bubbled up and split down her cheeks. *How can I put my child in a situation of unending suffering through hate or fear?* She was in no state to consider the alternative, but with sudden conviction she spoke. "He's mine. I must keep him, care for him. No matter what he goes through, we will go through it together."

"We understand, but if you change your mind we're here to help. You've been of immense assistance and we appreciate it."

"What do you mean by 'immense assistance?'"

The man seemed happy to explain. "You were chosen for the privilege of producing an offspring in which DNA engineering is being used to produce humans with certain reptilian qualities. It has been established that after any nuclear explosion tests they are the sole survivors."

His voice took on the proud tone of a fanatic with a cause. "We, under the guidance of the High One, have the glorious duty of combining certain qualities in reptiles with the DNA in humans, otherwise, with the increase in radiation the human race is doomed. You have been of great value in our cause. Of course, it's only in the experimental stages at present, but all offspring are living happy lives in another addition to this... complex. They will one day rule the world after the present human species have destroyed themselves, and almost everything on it. Your son will be instrumental as a leader in this new world, which will have to be recreated out of chaos."

Newina gained the impression he wanted her approval, or

worst, her thanks for being part of this bizarre experiment. *Perhaps it's all some kind of joke, or hoax?*

The second man added. "Your child is the first male child produced. He'll be named Mada, reverse for Adam, appropriate as the first Adam was the leader of a new civilisation and so will Mada be. We are returning to the beginning."

"No, no, not my baby...no! He's mine!" Newina shouted over and over. She became hysterical, swinging her body and trying to get out of the bed. She was quickly sedated.

She remained in a drug-induced fog for several days. She finally woke with a clear mind to find herself back in her resort bed with Elam seated on a chair beside the bed. The sun had set and it was now dusk.

She wanted answers and her words came out in a rush. "Where is my baby?"

"Be calm Newina. The nurse will bring him over shortly."

"I want him here with me."

Elam nodded "I know," he said quietly.

"Tell me this Elam. Is DNA engineering behind what's going on here? I work in a laboratory and I know that Professor Whimsy has been carrying out a few secret experiments we are not part of. Are they connected to this place?"

Elam sat silently as she continued in a rush. "I would like to know whether Professor Whimsy and Professor Foster are involved. They are the ones responsible for me being here." Newina drew herself into a sitting position and leaned towards Elam. "Also tell me. Are aliens involved somehow?"

"I'm sorry, but I cannot answer you. With the infants who are here though, their mothers never wanted them or, like Una, nor even see them. In your case you came out of the anaesthetic too early. You were to be told your child had died, as we are extremely aware of the consequences of taking such a child with you, into what would be a hostile world for him. He would be considered a monstrosity, but here he is destined to be a great leader in the new world...the second Adam."

Controlling her rising anger Newina glared at him. "I am his mother. We will face whatever comes, together. I will love him and he will love me. We will be happy."

"As you wish, but if it becomes too much, you can bring him to us. The children here are safe and well cared for. Women devoted to the children raise them and no doubt spoil them as well.

"I'll like to leave…go home as soon as possible."

"I thought you might, so I have arranged transport. It is waiting. You will be back in your flat by tomorrow morning." He rose to his feet. "Ring when you are ready to leave and I will have Mada ready for the journey."

Revol carried Newina's luggage and helped her settle in the back seat of the van. It's motor was revving up and Newina was becoming very impatient at the delay, when Revol returned with a large basket covered by fine netting. He placed it on the front seat beside the driver.

'The seat belts in the front are more secure. He is asleep and you will be home soon."

Before she could protest the van was moving. She soon felt listless and as she drifted into sleep she began to wonder if her constant sleep pattern was artificially induced.

....

Newina woke with the morning sun shining through the window of her flat. She lay between the covers of her own bed. She felt distressed. Her hands automatically felt the bed beside her. She was alone. Her body seemed lighter. *Did I have another nightmare I can't remember?* She shook off the nagging thought, rose, and put coffee on to brew. She decided to go to the bank. The rent had to be paid and food had to be bought. She poured herself coffee and drank it slowly,

At the bank the teller took her bankbook, stamped it, then handed it back with the cash she wanted. Newina glanced at the latest balance. She frowned – her account contained an extra $80,000 – an amount she would require if purchasing her own residence. She sighed and held her book ready to hand back to the teller. "There's some mistake. I didn't put this $80,000 in."

"No mistake. Someone from your solicitor's office deposited the money in your account. I remember because I handled it. He said it was a surprise legacy. He said you were away. Yes, a legacy, he said. I must say I was surprised he spoke like that. That's breaking confidentiality. They don't talk ever…strictly business you know… always in a hurry."

$80,000 – Was that a payment… for Mada? Newina backed away. *Mada? Where did that name come from? I don't know any Mada, and I have no solicitor.* In a stupor she bumped her way to the door. *She instinctively knew without reason that she would never be able to locate the solicitor, nor would anyone reclaim the money.*

She stumbled as she stepped outside. Confused, she sank down on to the low cement wall adjacent to the steps. *Mada, my poor Mada!* Tears came into her eyes as she stared unseeing at the curious passerbys. *Why am I crying? What's wrong with me?*

Her body barely reacted as a familiar voice spoke. She looked up, into the face of Lionel Foster. "It's all right Newina. You're still not well. You've been very sick, at times I believe in a coma. Come, I'll take you home. When we get there I want you to toss out that pile of science-fiction videos you keep watching and buy some Mills and Boon romances. They might help my cause."

Blindly she stood, swaying slightly. He tucked her arm under his to support her, and she walked beside him like a robot, back to her flat and a lifetime of strange dreams. Some included Lionel, sometimes as a lover, other times as a shadowy figure causing fear.

WAS IT BLACK?

THE NEWSREADER on radio station 4UR announced:
"At 4.20 this morning, traffic was chaotic on the Bruce Highway, 20 kilometres north of Brisbane, when a truck enroute to the Northgate Cannery lost its load of ripe tomatoes while rounding a bend during heavy rain. Several motorists skidded on the slippery mess and a few minor incidents occurred. The police are now directing traffic around the pileup and the highway should be back to normal by 7.30. A fire engine has been called in to hose the tonnes of squashed tomatoes from the wet road. Actual cause of the incident is unknown at present."

....

Just before 4.20a.m, the driver, Steve Anderson, sitting in the cabin of the semi-trailer, tried to stretch his long cramped body in an effort to get some relief from the effects of four hours of constant driving. His wife Helen had not wanted him to take the truck, but his mate, semi-trailer driver Austin, asked him to deliver his load of ripe tomatoes to the city as he was too sick and would not make it.

Steve's eyes squinted to see the road through the blurred rain-lashed windscreen as a smile played upon his generous mouth while he recalled Helen pointing out that he had not driven such a large vehicle for at least a year. She also reminded him it was pouring rain and the roads would be slippery. He remembered saying, 'Got to help me mate out,' and with a quick peck on her cheek had climbed into the truck and driven away.

After driving in the rain and dark for four hours he was growing tired and impatient to return home, where he knew Helen would have a hot meal and warm dry clothes laid out for him.

His heavy boot eased off the accelerator as a bend showed ahead. It was still raining and visibility was low. As he steered the truck around it he squinted through the blurred windscreen at a movement on the road directly ahead. He braked immediately. A drenched form narrowly missed by the truck's wheels streaked past his vision and out of sight.

He felt the tyres refuse to grip on to the wet bitumen and loose gravel. He tried desperately to control the vehicle. The truck come to a sudden body-shaking halt as it skidded on to the sloping shoulder of the road. A loud protest from the motor joined up with the sound of splintering wood as his load slipped to one side and boxes tumbled off, scattering and breaking open – their contents splattering and spreading over both lanes.

Shaking, but now in control of his nerves Steve clambered down from the cabin, wondering if what he had missed hitting was safe.

Surveying the sea of spreading pulp from the broken boxes and the banking up of cars he swore. *Bloody hell! Wait 'til I see Austin. I thought the ropes had not been strong enough or tight enough, but Austin had disagreed with me. I've a score to settle with him when I get back.*

He could hear a police siren. *Some panicking driver in one of those cars skating on the slippery bitumen must have called the police. What can I say to them...that I lost control on the wet bitumen because I jammed on the brakes to avoid something that was running across the road in front of the truck – a cat that looked just like my little daughter's?*

NO, NEVER!

CHILD NEEDS A PADDLING

I KNOW what it is to be up the creek without the proverbial paddle, subject to tide, wind and a Queensland summer sun. Whose idea was it to go canoeing when lack of balance is my inherited trait?

Be careful when giving in to grandsons is my advice, or you could be up the creek without a paddle as I was, when persuaded to step into a small wobbly canoe.

He said, 'Isn't it great Gran?' as he held the side of the canoe while still standing beside it in the water. He was dressed in his togs and doting me believed he would get into the canoe with me, but I should have twigged. He then gave the canoe a mighty shove. I was hardly seated. Gripping the side I glanced around and wondered where the oars were. 'I'm not sure I like this. It's too shaky,' I told him. *'Now where did he go?'* He was nowhere to be seen.

On floated the darn thing with me in it, clutching the sides. Then through an arch of trees that crisscrossed above reflected gnarled trees and scrubs it slowly went. Then around a slight bend I drifted. I tried to convince myself I wasn't scared, especially when a bunch of noisy minors, objecting to my presence, gathered on the nearest treetop and stared at me. Several crows were watching me but lost interest quickly and moved on... their carking loud enough to wake the dead.

A bolt of colour escaping from the under-wings of a dozen rainbow parakeets dipped and soared low overhead. I ducked my head. 'Don't you come too close,' I told them.

A kookaburra laughed at me. 'Funny? I don't think,' I muttered back.

Then something stirred beneath the boat... a crocodile? 'Of course not... too far south,' I told myself, but did wonder if this creek eventually ended in the sea. Then the current seemed to be getting stronger. I was heading into a whirly, straight towards the bank. I asked myself fearfully, 'Why are there no oars and if there were how would you row the thing, or stop it, or turn around?'

Frozen stiff with fright I closed my eyes and braced myself

for the end, believing I was going to drown. I regretted not learning to swim when I was a kid, those many years ago.

The boat tilted to one side. If there were crocodiles this far south, or sharks, why did my grandson put me into this thing? I wondered this with my eyes shut tight. Nothing happened so I half opened them. I was still dreading the worst when a head popped up beside the canoe. It was Roger. I was sweating with relief. I was saved.

"How's Gran? Great isn't it?" the silly child asked.

I twitched my face into a forced smile to make like I was happy as can be.

He said. 'Sorry to run off like that but I almost lost my shorts. The elastic's had its day. I had to go back and put another one on." He laughed then. "The custom you know, but no sweat, the river's only waist deep, and, you only went a few yards from where I left you."

I felt I could have strangled him, but revenge would come later.

TOBY TO THE RESCUE

KENNETH ROSS PULLED ON TOBY'S LEAD as the fox terrier loitered at the corner. It was already nine-thirty and it concerned him to think that Melody may have left.

When he entered the park he was breathless as he dragged the reluctant Toby, who wanted to sniff every post, to his usual seat, from where he could watch Melody as she walked the park picking up autumn leaves, while humming at the same time.

On each visit he had watched Melody and now knew her route. He had given her that name because she had long blonde hair that suited her small face, and she was light on her feet, but mostly because she hummed popular songs. She walked with a grace he had noticed on no one else. She gave him the impression of floating as she carried a small basket into which she dropped the autumn leaves. He was drawn to her as he was drawn to no other woman. He knew that now he had seen her, her memory and what might have been, would distract him all his life if he did not get to meet her. She was like a pleasant dream that you wanted to come true. Kenneth was, for the first time, in love.

He had tried to catch her eye once but she had immediately turned her head. He decided he must think of a better way.

He could not bring himself to openly stare at her as some others did, and who muttered quietly as she passed, yet, like them, he too wondered why this pretty, petite young girl, who always wore a serious expression on her face, would come to a park to collect freshly fallen leaves several days a week.

He recalled that, when a child, he and the other children in his class had a craze for pressing flowers and leaves and gluing them on to paper to make bookmarks, or inside their exercise books. But Melody did not look like a mother. *No!* He dismissed the thought. *She could work at a school, but schools never collected children's playthings. The children did that themselves.*

Kenneth sat down and opened his magazine, bought especially for the purpose of holding it in such a way that Melody would not realise he was watching her. He now half hid his face as Toby pulled on his lead. With a merry laugh Kenneth bent over and released him. Toby scampered away, to tumble headlong into the first hole in the ground. Kenneth's smile remained as he mentally visualised his landlady's expression if she could see Toby off the leash.

She had been given Toby recently. After pulling a muscle in her leg she had trouble walking. She decided Kenneth should be the one to take him for his early morning walks to the nearby park until her leg had healed enough for her to take over.

On the first day Kenneth had consented reluctantly, claiming that night work entitled him to rest during the day. He secretly thought that only old ladies looked good walking with puppies trotting along beside them. Mrs Daly had also strictly forbidden him to let Toby roam free. 'Because,' she had said while stroking its stomach in a farewell gesture, 'the poor little dear might get lost or run over, or bite someone. He's often tries to bite my ankles, and has ruined a couple of my shoes in the process.' This gave Kenneth an idea.

He now glanced around and noticed Melody heading in his direction. She was directly in his line of vision when she stopped before a Liquid Amber tree with multi-coloured autumn leaves in abundance. He held the open magazine higher, but low enough for him to watch her. As she came closer he looked sideways to the ground, searching for Toby. He faintly smiled as he saw Toby eyeing Melody. He crossed his fingers hoping Toby would not fail him. He quietly said. "Go Toby go."

Toby on cue scampered towards Melody, eyeing her ankles and growling joyously. He playfully gripped the back of one of Melody's shoes as Kenneth had been encouraging him to do. Melody gave a low cry of surprise and tried to shake Toby off, but he kept a firm hold.

Kenneth threw his magazine aside and hurried over to her. He pulled Toby away and held him to his chest. Toby licked Kenneth's face, expecting the usual reward. When he received no titbit he tried to jump to the ground but Kenneth held him tighter. "I'm so sorry. Did he hurt you?"

"No, I'm all right thank you," came the answer as she examined the teeth marks on the back of one of her shoes.

Her voice was as Kenneth had expected, soft and musical. He thought he had named her well.

"Perhaps I can walk you home. It's the least I can do, and I'll be there if you have trouble with that shoe."

"Thank you." The easy reply was the opposite of what Kenneth had expected.

He settled the wriggling pup under one arm. He became quiet, sulking perhaps after his short-lived freedom. With his other hand Kenneth took the basket from Melody. When she did not protest Kenneth was thrilled. He thought it was easier than he had imagined and could have kicked himself for the time he had wasted. But his exaltation was short-lived for she added, "Only to the corner of Barlow Street thanks. I have work to do."

'Picking up more leaves,' thought Kenneth dryly, but he said, "Anywhere you say, Melody."

"Melody?" Her eyes widened in surprise.

"Yes, I've seen you here quite often, and felt I had to give you a name, and Melody suited you so well. You're not offended?"

"No, I like it."

"Unless you'd prefer me to use your right name. Mine's Kenneth, Kenneth Ross."

"Kenneth, I thought it would be Jim or Bob; something short."

"So you did notice me." Kenneth's delight was obvious; although he was slightly peeved she had avoided telling him her name.

"I couldn't help it," was the reply. "You are about the only person who doesn't stare rudely at me wondering why I bother to collect leaves."

Kenneth thought he must write to someone and congratulate them for inventing the magazine he used to hide behind.

"Well," he said, "It's a little unorthodox for a beautiful young woman to keep coming to a park to pick up a basket full of common leaves from equally common trees."

To his surprise and annoyance, Melody laughed softly but

offered no explanation. Kenneth felt let down and assumed he was really getting nowhere.

She looked at her watch. "I must go now."

Quickly attaching the strap to Toby's collar, together they left the park. After walking past several streets she stopped as they drew near the corner of Barlow Street. She turned to face him. "This is where I leave you."

"Oh...no further?" Kenneth was genuinely disappointed. He felt he was still no closer to getting to know her.

"Goodbye and thank you," she said as she turned to walk down Barlow Street. Suddenly she stopped and turned to face him again. "My name is Belinda Fletcher...'bye." Before he could think of a suitable reply she was out of sight.

He waited for what he thought was a sufficiently safe period, then, tossing away the butt of his cigarette, he walked quickly into Barlow Street. He was in time to see Melody disappear through a gate at the front of a tall white building.

He hurried. On reaching the fence surrounding the property, he whistled softly as he read a large sign attached to it. The mystery of Melody's daily visit to the park was solved.

Kenneth felt extremely content as he strolled away, sure now of his success with Melody.

"From now on Toby," he said. "We'll help Melody pick up leaves." Toby looked at Kenneth with a begging expression, then flopped down across Kenneth's boots.

"Okay, you win." Kenneth drew out a dog biscuit. Toby jumped up, propping his paws against Kenneth's knees, to snatch it from Kenneth's fingers. Kenneth's mind drifted back to Melody as he waited while Toby enjoyed his reward.

Ten months later Kenneth and Belinda were married. Toby, with a black bow tie attached to the front of his collar, walked beside the bridesmaids into the church.

Before the wedding Melody made it very clear to Kenneth that, regardless of any ideas he might have that every woman belonged mainly in the kitchen, she was going to continue her work as a teacher at the Sunshine Home for Crippled Children.

GET A LIFE

HER TEMPLES THUMPED and her nerves danced with excitement as Hester drooled over the shiny new cars in the car sales yard. Racked with indecision she wandered around until she spied a gleaming sports car. She went to examine its new modern features, and bright yellow colour.

"YOU want to buy a Honda Sports car?" queried the smiling, smooth-voiced salesman; while his eyebrows raised as he scrutinized her well-past middle-age spreading figure and her lined face. "Or is if for your son?"

Hester gave him a look of disgust. "No, for me."

He was not intimidated. "Are you sure? Perhaps you would like to see a 4 cyl Mazda sedan instead?"

"I AM sure," Hester snapped. How else was she to 'get a life', something her grandson Darren now living with her, kept impressing on her. She knew he believed she was cemented solidly in the grief that dominated her life since her husband of thirty-five years died. "All this living in the past Grandma makes you old and out of touch." was the message he imparted to her.

I'll show him. "I'll take it."

The deal was finally completed, and Hester smoothed down the sides of her loose red dress as she climbed into her new car. The seat hugged her body as if made to order for her. The steering wheel was dimpled and turned at a light caress. The acceleration was a dream. Trees flashed past as she drove without glancing at the speedometer. It was so exhilarating. Wind tore at her hair.

"Wow!" she exclaimed as she went faster still as unconscious pressure from her heavy thick-soled sandals forced down the accelerator. "Now I've got a life," she shouted with joy.

Suddenly her vision was dominated by the switching on of the red stoplight at an intersection, which seemed to appear out of nowhere. The car was going too fast to stop and too fast to swerve in time to avoid oncoming traffic.

A red truck of seemingly huge dimensions was shooting directly at her. She felt the straps of her sandals cut into her foot as she braked hard. Her mind, stunned with shock, now recognized the inevitable – the crash of protective metal – the crushing sound of breaking glass.

Her body jolted with pain while splinters of glass pierced her flesh. Mechanically her fingers found the clasp of her seat belt, quickly releasing it's grip on her chest. She was too stunned for tears. She reached for the door handle. It was jammed and refused to open. Her legs felt like jelly. Pain jabbed at her back and her arms stung from bleeding cuts. She tasted blood as she desperately wriggled her body on to the passenger seat.

'Thank God,' she thought as the door swung open to her thrust. She gingerly twisted herself further to slide out. Grasping the top of the open door she managed to stand while leaning on the bonnet of the car, but could not stop the uncontrollably jumbled and confused thoughts racing around in her brain. She became disorientated. She tried hard to focus on a stocky grey-haired man standing before her. Disbelief was etched on his craggy features.

"Are you all right?"

Hester's tongue stuck fast in her mouth. She made a sound, but it was nothing more than a whimper. Her legs suddenly doubled beneath her. As she fell she felt the pressure of strong arms trying to hold her upright, then she mercifully blacked out. She was unaware of the ambulance and the fast ride to the hospital where Hester endured the pain as her injuries slowly healed.

Her grandson on his first visit listened to her story. He said, "Sorry Grandma I didn't mean you to take me literally when I said 'get a life.' Hester sniffed loudly and refused to reply. He smiled as he rose to leave. He leaned over and whispered. 'I think you're cool." The biggest compliment Hester could expect from him.

Just you wait 'till I get home. I'll have him doing jobs about the house that he never knew existed, let alone needed doing. But she squeezed his hand as he said goodbye.

One morning the doctor's voice was a delight to her ears. "Hester Hooper, you are free to leave the hospital whenever you wish."

"Thanks. I'll get ready and wait for Steve. He's coming soon. He'll take me home."

The doctor smiled. "Oh yes, Steve, the other driver who came in with you but was not badly hurt, and has been a constant visitor since."

An hour later when Hester, aided by Steve, walked to his waiting car, she knew that, with grey-haired Steve on the way to being entrenched in her life, she would never again be intimidated into "getting a life." She knew she already had one, and first thing tomorrow she would get rid of the red sports car.

LETTER OF DESTINY

THE JASMINE CREEPER that wound in and out of the suburban fence threw delicate fragrance into the air as distraught eighteen-year old Sylvia, dressed in her lightweight shower-proof coat against the cool autumn air hurried past. Instead of inhaling the intoxicating perfume as she usually did, tears blurred her vision and she failed to notice anything about the familiar street. Her mind was overwhelmed by soul-wrenching disappointment, coloured by disbelief.

Adrian's letter was now crushed in her coat pocket. When she read it she had wanted to die. Now she had the urge to run away, to escape from a world that seemed to give her only grief and unhappiness. The immediate reaction after reading her fiancée's letter was shock, which slowly drained from her the will to live. 'Death would be a peaceful release,' she decided.

Her unblemished, heart-shaped face with its delicate small bones gave her an elfin look, but now it was shiny and red, smothered with smeared make-up from constantly wiping away the tears. Her blue eyes were blood streaked under swollen lids. Her hair was dishevelled with many small blonde strands glued to her face.

As her mind became more distraught with mixed anger and hurt, tears trembled on her long eyelashes. With her unseeing gaze directed towards the bitumen road under foot she walked quickly onwards.

One gloved hand clutched the lapels of her long light coat in an effort to keep out the cool air. The other was now inside its single pocket, clutching the crumbled letter and her small purse. Her fingers were stiff with the cold jabbing at her fingers through her thin gloves. The gloves had been part of her high school uniform, and suddenly she pictured her old life in the small country town. She painfully relived the end of her secure and happy home life. She recalled the nervous policeman standing at the door, who had held her against him as she almost collapsed when told that her parents had been killed in a car accident.

Their funeral was a blur in her mind even then, but throughout the horror of it all she had her fiance Adrian to lean on. Adrian had been her only boyfriend. He had been a rock of safety and comfort in her time of desolation. Later, when he told her he had accepted a temporary transfer in his job to New Guinea she had felt sick, but in the dazzling light of his enthusiasm, she had let him go unhindered by any display of her inward doubts.

She recalled his suggestion she move to the city and wait for him there.

'When I come back I will be stationed in Brisbane so why not be there when I return?' She agreed and resigned from her job to move to Brisbane. 'I know the days will go slowly, but I will make up for it my precious love. A year will go fast and I will come back with enough money saved to buy our own home. We'll be married immediately and live happily ever after....' He had told her this, unmindful of the extent of the loneliness that even then had begun to creep over her.

His weekly letters were full of endearing terms of how much he missed her, and always finished with, 'All my love forever.... I can't wait to hold you in my arms.' But now those words were bitter gall to swallow. It was now over. She had not received a letter for two weeks. Now she knew why. He was never coming back. Sylvia felt herself plunged deeper into a well of sorrow and despair, and to Sylvia the well seemed bottomless.

"How could he? How could he?" she cried aloud. The tears flowed unchecked as she stumbled forward through the now lifting fog, unaware she was no longer walking on the footpath but on the edge of the roadway. She was deaf to the blast of horns directed at her by alarmed drivers. The fog continued to envelope her, and the narrow echo of the tap tap of her high-heeled shoes on her long slim well-proportioned legs, rose and fell in rhythm.

She kept following the road that led to the park. She was not conscious of why she was heading in that direction, only that she wanted to be away from her cold, lonely flat. *What better place than to be in the park I love, where I feed the pigeons every day and watch the dark oily river slip by, oblivious of time.*

She entered the park through a shortcut to the river itself. Tiny stones flung up by her shoes, crashed themselves against her ankles, but the subsequent sting on her legs remained unnoticed.

She reached the river and stopped under the low branches of a Poinciana tree close to the bank. She stared at the water, gurgling as it moved and splashed against the brick retaining wall and slithered over the grassy edge. It mesmerised her. An old forgotten bench leaned against the tree at a drunken angle. Sylvia lowered her light body on to it. She sighed a deep shuddering sigh as her thoughts remained consumed by her conviction that life was not worth living. With her mum and dad dead, no job, turned down or discouraged at every effort to find work, no friends, little money, and now, with Adrian gone, she was all alone. *No one cares whether I'm alive or dead.*

'How could he?' she half whispered and the tears that had momentarily dried were again ready to be released. 'How could he fall in love with someone else?' she demanded in vain. *He has always loved me and I him. How could he write that our love belonged to the past? He vowed we would be together always, even after death. Who is this terrible heartless woman, this selfish horrible...horrible bitch! No decent woman would steal another's fiancée. She must have known we were engaged to be married."*

She drew out the crumpled letter and smoothed it out with both hands, desperately hoping that somehow she had read it incorrectly, but she knew she had not as she again read.

'I won't be coming back. I will always love you Sylvia, but my love for Danielle is so strong, so different. We will be married here and stay in New Guinea. Please try to understand, if not now, you will when you too meet your soul mate, your real true love.'

"Real true love? Wasn't ours real true love?" she sobbed aloud.

She crunched the letter into a ball and cast it to the ground.

Nervously she rose and walked slowly to the river's edge. She leaned forward. *I have nothing to live for. No one will miss me, absolutely no one*. She stepped closer but hesitated. She took a step to one side and her foot slipped on the wet grassy edge of the river. She gave a soft cry of surprise as she felt herself falling.

The water opened with a splash of protest as Sylvia's weight slipped through. The shock of the sudden biting cold passed through her body, and her whole being shuddered for some seconds until she became immune to it. Treading water she slipped out of her coat. For several seconds it was tossed about by the current, and then disappeared from her view. Her shoes had slipped from her feet. Her remaining clothes were heavy but she was a good swimmer and they were not a great hindrance as she began to float on the water's surface, letting the current take her slowly down stream.

Deep in her despair, she was unaware of the city lights, or of the voices coming from the bridge as she floated closer to it. Obsessed by the thought of Adrian, his face seemed to dance in front of her, to be replaced by those of her parents. They seemed to be trying to tell her something. Guilt edged its way into her soul. She knew she could reach the bank if she tried.

Why am I floating instead of letting the current take me under? The question formed in her mind. Did she doubt the wisdom of her intention? She wondered how long it would be before she grew too tired to keep herself afloat. She knew her parents would have wanted her not to give up. She pushed the thought aside.

Sylvia, without conscious effect had been vaguely aware of a blurred form of a child moving on the bridge ahead. Suddenly, above the muffled sound of distant traffic, a child's scream pierced the fog. Then Sylvia made out a small figure falling. A loud splash followed as the child made contact with the water, which opened to encase her.

All else forgotten, she instinctively swam towards the child. She reached the child as the current was tossing the small body up and then under in playful tumbles. Sylvia treaded water as she grabbed the child's coat and drew her closer. Having learnt life-saving skills at school, she turned the child on her back to avoid the grasping arms which would drew her under also. She placed one arm under the child's chin to keep her face above water and swam with her slowly towards the bank as the water strained to keep them in its grasp.

She was exhausted when she reached the safety of the bank. She became aware of arms reaching down to take the child from her, then she felt herself being dragged up the muddy bank on to grass. Her knees scraped on something hard and she was not long conscious of anything around her.

When Sylvia finally woke, she found herself gazing into the concerned features of a tall, handsome, dark haired, muscled man with the darkest blue eyes she had ever seen. Deep concern was etched into his expressive features.

"Where am I?" she asked, trying to rise, but a gentle hand pushed her down again on to the bed.

"In our house. I am Paul and this is my sister Cindy, mother of Elena, the child you saved."

Sylvia focused her eyes on Cindy who was remarkably like her brother in looks. She then noticed another – an older man standing to one side.

The young man turned to him. "Will she be all right doctor?" he asked.

"It's hard to tell," he replied. "She has no serious injuries. Her knees are scraped but the cuts are not deep. She has a temperature, and is suffering from shock. She could be in for pneumonia and should stay in bed and keep warm. I'll call again at this time tomorrow."

"No, no, I can't stay here. I must go," Sylvia protested. She tried to rise again but this time the doctor pushed her gently back down. He turned to Cindy. "I've given her a sedative. Keep her in bed for the present. She can't be moved in the state she's in."

"She can stay here as long as she likes. If it weren't for her, Elena would have been swept away and drowned. Anyway we don't know her name or where she's from."

He turned to Sylvia who felt her eyelids were too heavy to keep open.

"What is your name young lady, and your address?"

"Sylvia," she whispered. She mumbled her address as she felt herself falling into a deep drugged sleep while the doctor continued. "If she is kept warm and takes the medicine she should be all right. Ring me if you have any problems."

"Thanks Doctor. We will."

She only faintly heard footsteps and a door closing as she sunk into oblivion.

The following day Sylvia felt her whole body was burning. She drifted in and out of consciousness. Several times she called Paul, 'Adrian'. Other times she asked if Adrian had arrived yet, then immediately appeared disinterested and relaxed back into a trance-like state. During those times when her mind cleared and she began to think rationally, she realised she had failed miserably to end her life. *I was entertaining the thought even before I slipped in. I'm nothing but a coward. I kept floating. Perhaps the fever will do it for me. What have I got to live for now? I'm better off dead.* The dark depression that possessed her seemed to fall to even greater depths.

On other days when she appeared brighter Paul and Cindy's show of gratitude embarrassed her. They treated her as a heroine, which she knew in her heart she was not. *But I don't expect to be here very long so it doesn't matter what they think.*

Elena insisted on showing her toys to Sylvia and chatting away to her. As dark thoughts remained to torment her, a feeling of resentment rose towards the one who prevented her from ending the misery she was in. But as she recovered, the kindness shown by the family became a pleasure, and she was able to return their good humour and companionship, and Elena's company was a joy.

Although she was fast regaining her strength she knew she would be reluctant to leave. From the time she was well enough, she responded happily to Paul's obvious interest in her. Her whole body would thrill to his touch when he held her hand to steady her on her feet as she recovered. Looking into her eyes the space created between them seemed electric. It created the feeling of belonging that she hungered for, and was surprised to find thoughts of Adrian beginning to recede, no longer carrying the same intensity of hurt and anger. But a feeling of guilt from believing she was betraying her own feelings for Adrian quickly squashed the romantic feelings trying to gain life. She had blamed

Adrian for deserting her, now it seemed to her, she was deserting his memory and the love she herself had believed would last through life and beyond.

When she and Paul were alone in the house one evening, they sat together on the cane divan on the veranda watching the lights of the city. Paul moved closer to Sylvia. She did not move away but said sadly, "I'll have to be leaving soon."

She felt Paul's arm encircling her shoulders. She turned her head away from him, aware of a rush of blood to her face, and feeling embarrassed at her longing for him to hold her in his arms.

"Do you mind Sylvia?"

Sylvia did not trust herself to answer.

Paul took the silence to mean she did not, and his arms tightened around her.

"I know you must go some time Sylvia, but I'll miss you. I hate the thought of you leaving. You're part of the family now." He hesitated before continuing. "Sylvia, I must ask you this. What are your feelings towards me? Do I get a look in? Is there anyone else?" he enquired earnestly.

Sylvia kept her head turned away, confused by mixed feelings of longing for Paul and bad memories that crowded in upon her, making her fearful of making even the slightest commitment.

When she did not reply Paul's fingers reached up and turned her face to him. He looked steadily, searchingly, into her eyes, his own full of hope. All her fears dissolved.

"I can see in your eyes that you feel as I do. So do I get a 'yes'?"

"Yes," Sylvia's voice was soft and breathless. Paul, delighted, clasped her tightly to him and kissed her forcefully, expressing the extent of his pent up emotions. It lasted a long time and thrilled her whole being. She did not want it to end. When their lips parted she asked herself if this was what Adrian meant when he wrote about true love and soul mates, then melted back into Paul's arms filled with a greater happiness then she had ever known. Adrian's love had been a sweet placid relationship, a belonging dominated by a feeling of knowing that life with him would have been contentment and happy protection. With Paul, love included excitement and an intensity and depth of feeling new to Sylvia.

"I have a surprise for you. I'm putting your name up for a citation for bravery when the Government awards come up shortly."

Suddenly Sylvia froze and all the pain of the past returned.

"You must not, " she implored. "I'm not a hero. I just did what I had to do."

"Don't be silly. You deserve it. I won't hear any more objections." He bent to kiss her again but the rapture of the night was gone. She rose.

"Goodnight Paul."

Before he could speak she was in her bedroom. She threw herself on the bed and wept in despair. *If he knew it was by sheer chance that I saved Elena he would hate me. I have to leave.*

A sad Sylva, physically and mentally exhausted from tossing and turning all night, was relieved when dawn arrived. She knew what she must do. Firstly she wrote a letter of thanks to Paul and his sister, and then quickly dressed and quietly left the house.

She took a taxi back to her flat. The caretaker was pleased to see her and asked if she had enjoyed her stay away. She did not enlighten him but took the letter he was holding out to her. She looked at the envelope and she knew it was from the firm where her job application and subsequent interview had been unsuccessful. Curious, she opened it, and read.

'. . . As previously advised, you were not successful in your job application as a secretary in our main office. However, in two months' time the plant will be expanded and our staff requirements will naturally increase, so we have pleasure in offering you a similar position to the one for which you applied, with training to start on the first of next month. The position is yours, should you be still interested . . ."

It was the type of job she wanted and should have been thrilled, but it was too late. She felt she must leave. In a fit of frustration she threw the letter into the waste paper basket. *I'll go back to Gympie and start anew.* She could not deny that she would never completely stop the feelings she had for both Adrian and Paul, but convinced herself a new start would make those feelings dissipate as time went by.

He would have nothing to do with me anyway if he knew I was not the brave person he thinks I am. This is the only way. She choked at the thought. *But I must be honest and explain to him why I left so suddenly. I'll write it in a letter to him and that will be that. I won't be seeing him again.*

She sat down to write immediately. Intending to write a short note she found herself pouring out her feelings from the time her parents were killed, to her thoughts about suicide. She explained how much she felt for him but how impossible it was to develop a relationship based on her immature, no, childish reaction to the disappointments she was experiencing. She explained that at the time it seemed a possible and perhaps only way out of the suffering she was going through. She begged him to forgive her for letting him and Cindy think she was a heroine. She sealed the envelope but found she had no stamp. She would post the letter when she arrived at Gympie.

She packed immediately and left for the station. As she waited on the platform she began to miss Paul already. Dismay set in as she became convinced once again that she was doomed to a life of unhappiness and misery. In her mind nothing seemed to be turning out right. She felt very alone. It seemed an eternity had passed when she heard the guard announce that the train was due in one minute. She gathered her belongings and moved to the edge of the platform.

With the rasping sound of wheels and hissing of escaping air the train came to a smooth stop. The automatic doors opened directly in front of Sylvia, but as she placed one foot on the entrance step, a firm hand gripped her upper arm. She was pulled back, away from the train.

She turned and gasped, "Paul! No Paul, I must go. Please leave me alone," she implored him, although her heart was beating faster at the sight of him. He kept his grip on her arm until the train doors closed.

"How did you know where to find me?" she asked.

"After last night I thought you might decide to leave. When I found you gone I drove to your address but got caught up in traffic on the way. When I got there the caretaker told me you had left to catch the Gympie train. It seems I got here just in time."

He still held on to her arm tightly as if frightened she would escape him and guided her to a seat on the now empty station. Dropping his arm he turned to face her. The look of concern on his face made Sylvia want to throw herself into his arms, but without speaking she searched in her bag and found the letter. She handed it to him. *This will be final. He'll willingly let me go after he reads it.*

"This will explain why I have to leave," she told him

Sylvia could not look at him and turned away, beginning to regret how she had unburdened her soul in that letter. He read it quickly.

"You poor darling." He spoke gently, sincerely.

Sylvia was both amazed and startled at his reaction. "You don't hate me for deceiving you and Cindy?"

"You silly girl. We knew all the time."

"Knew, but how? Did I talk too much when I was out to it?"

"Of course not, but when we knew, we were hoping you would tell us of your own accord."

"But how did you know?"

"Well, you had no identification on you so we went looking for a handbag or something. We thought it might be washed up on the bank or in the mud when the tide was out. All we found was a discarded letter and a soggy coat in the mud that had a purse and flat key in it. That's how we knew your address. You tried to tell us your address but we didn't understand what you were saying, and you were very sick during the next few days. That letter we found, also mentioned your parents' demise so we knew what you were going through.

Cindy and I both thought it strange when we heard a splash before Elena fell in. Afterwards I knew it must have been you, and after reading the letter I put two and two together. Knowing you, if you had not slipped in, I don't believe you would have actually jumped in and drowned. You proved you were a good swimmer when you saved Elena."

Sylvia began to feel ashamed for hiding everything from them, but before she could speak, Paul's face drew closer to hers. His closeness made her want to fall into his arms. She wanted to feel strength and comfort from his nearness.

"I want you to stay," he continued. "I think I've fallen in love with you, and it has nothing to do with gratitude either. Will you stay?"

"Oh Paul," Sylvia said softly, thinking how wonderful his eyes, filled with adoration and devotion, were, and she was thrilled with the pleasure only love could create.

"You will stay?"

"Yes," said Elena. He kissed her lightly on the lips, but she quickly drew her face away and thoughtfully said, "Thinking about it I don't think I would have stayed too long in that cold water even if I had jumped in instead of slipping in on the mud. At the time though, I thought life had nothing but misery for me." She hesitated. "But now I realise how lucky I really am. I have a job to go to, a new family, and most of all, you."

"Come on home then." He retrieved her suitcase, and with a protective arm around her, they walked out of the station to a future full of promise.

THE OTHER WOMAN

"NOW WHO CAN THAT BE ringing me now?" Jeanne asked herself irritably on her way the laundry. She dumped the bundle of soiled clothes on to the kitchen floor. She then leaned across the workbench to reach for the telephone.

If that's Donna again I'll scream. She was tired after a restless night and had already spent time that morning listening to her friend whingeing about her illnesses and her 'Harry doesn't love me any more' problem. Donna was obsessed with the belief that her husband was unfaithful, although she had not yet found anything concrete to back it up. Jeanne tossed back her long black hair and placed the receiver to her ear.

"Jeanne! Is that you Jeanne?"

Jeanne's first impulse was to say 'What now!' but realised she had told Donna she could call her any time. They had known each other from college days.

"Are you there Jeanne?"

"Yes, yes," Jeanne quickly responded, realising Donna's voice expressed more than the usual tearful whining. A note of panic had entered it, with shades of anger weaved in as well. "What's happened? Are you all right?"

"I'm as right as I'm ever likely to be the way Harry treats me." The voice became more controlled. Jeanne knew this different tone meant something new had hatched in Donna's fertile imagination.

"There IS another woman." Jeanne could hear Donna's sob. "And to think of how good I am to him. I never say 'no', whatever he wants. You know." Her voice was pleading for support. "I do everything for him, even put his toothpaste on his toothbrush each morning to save him time." Her voice trailed off to finish in a loud sob, but almost instantly she regained her composure. "But I'm going to be civilised about this. I'm going to tell him it's over. I've had enough of him being unfaithful. I'll tell him I'm going – going home to mother. He can have her."

Resigned to having to hear Donna out she decided she

might as well be comfortable. Groping with her hand behind her she dragged the kitchen stool over to the breakfast bar and seated herself. She reached across to switch on the electric jug, then drew the box of tea bags and a cup towards her. *If it's going to be the usual long tirade I may as well be comfortable.*

"You sound as if you've found out something, so what is it?" she asked although she was beginning to lose interest. She had heard similar stories from Donna many times. All were false alarms existing only in Donna's imagination. Both she and Warren often wondered how Harry put up with the endless accusations and the loud bitter arguments that followed.

"Well." Donna's voice had become high-pitched. "I told you before, that I've always suspected he was with another women when he said he had to work late. I'd ring his office and there would be no answer. He claimed he never answered it as it interrupted his work. He can't fool me and I've told him that many times."

Gripping the receiver between chin and shoulder Jeanne poured the milk; added sugar to her newly brewed tea, and waited. "What's different this time?" She sipped the hot brew.

"Well, I have proof now." Donna's voice had a satisfied sound of someone saying, 'I told you so!'

Jeanne's interest was suddenly rekindled. Perhaps all those boring repetitive phone calls were not merely the result of Donna's obsessive jealousy. Harry certainly had a gleam in his eye as he scrutinised her female guests as they arrived at their monthly barbecues. Donna always refused to attend, making some excuse such as, 'too tired,' or 'not a drinker,' Sometimes it was 'People always make fools of themselves at drinking parties. It's disgusting,' and more. But to those who attended, their parties were laughter, and so much fun.

As memories flowed through her mind her free hand strayed. It travelled smoothly over the fabric of her tight jeans, over her hip, returning to caress her flat stomach. She surged with pleasure as she recalled the admiring glances her figure always attracted, especially from Harry. Suddenly she realised Donna was still speaking. She wondered what she had missed.

"...and they were hidden in his socks drawer, but he can't hide anything from me. That was where I found the pink lace handkerchief with the initial "J" embroidered on it as well."

Jeanne froze. *J...for Jeanne? Is Donna about to accuse me of being the other woman? Perhaps my aversion to using paper tissues is a mistake.* She tried to keep her voice as steady as possible and hoped Donna would take her reaction as nothing more than surprise. Swallowing, she said, "A lace hankie, maybe it's a drycleaner's mistake."

Donna ignored the suggestion. "When I found it, as well as the lipstick AND the pair of black panties I knew I was right about the rotten cheat all along."

Jeanne tried to keep her voice calm; possessed now with the added realisation the panties were hers. "I'm sure Harry would have a very good explanation. Of course there must be some simple explanation. I wish I could think of one to ease your mind but at the moment I can't. I just want to get on with my washing."

"Well! If your washing is more important than your best friend's troubles I'll go. Goodbye!" The bang at Donna's end as she slammed down the receiver vibrated through Jeanne's head.

Jeanne sat motionless with the dead receiver held in one hand and a cup of tea going cold in the other. "*Hankie? lipstick? black panties? They could be mine.* She began to picture not only losing her best friend if Donna accused her of being the 'other woman,' but her own marriage would be in trouble. Warren could be unforgiving if he thought he was being crossed. She wondered what Harry could possibly say to Donna who had already made up her mind, tried him and declared him guilty.

I'll have to warn him. She quickly dialled his work number with shaking fingers. *Perhaps he could say he found them?.... bought them for Donna?...Sales gimmick?...Left by a 'hopeful' in his office – now sacked. Hurry Harry! He has to be in.*

Then the call was through, but before Harry could say more than 'hello', she began. " Harry I've got to tell you what's happened." Jeanne breathlessly relayed all Donna had said before Harry could say anything. "And when she mentioned the lipstick, hankie and panties I just couldn't tell her that they were mine; that when we were dancing once I put the lipstick and hankie in your top pocket and forgot about them. Neither of us could tell Donna about the panties -- she wouldn't have accepted it anyway – that I bought them on the last party day. I was late home from shopping and out of time and I dropped the packet on the lounge chair intending to put them away as soon as I checked the finger food Warren was getting ready. Then I got busy and forgot.

Around mid-night, you remember, sticky-beak Gordon, full of grog, saw the packet and opened it. As a joke he decided to hold a competition. The winner was to be the one who told a joke that got the most laughs. It was a lot of fun at the time, but now in hindsight? You won, but why didn't you leave them behind? Were you too embarrassed to return them when you were sober? Whatever it was it won't help you now. Nothing's going to pacify Donna."

"Calm down Jeanne." To her surprise and amazement he sounded happy. "Thanks for letting me know. I knew it wouldn't take long for Donna to find them."

Jeanne gasped, "But why?"

"Now stop panicking. I'm not bringing you into it. Lots of women's names start with 'J'.

"But why did you keep them?"

"Jeanne, try to understand. It's the kindest way to end our marriage. It's been in name only for some time, and when I won those ...err...nice things of yours I got a brilliant idea. I know I'm a coward. I'm no match for Donna. I couldn't face the tirade I'd get if it came from me that our marriage was over, so I thought I would make her happy to think she was right about the 'other woman'. She's been complaining about a nonexistent 'other woman' for years, but believe me, if she doesn't go back to her mother, I won't be hanging around. I've had enough."

There was a pause, then he chuckled softly. "You realise don't you Jeanne that you're Donna's 'Other Woman'. By the way if you are interested in making it a reality. I'm game, if you are."

Jeanne wanted to crush the inviting tone in his voice but a snort was all she managed as she quickly banged down the receiver.

A REVOLVING DOOR

SIXTY-FIVE YEAR-OLD SHEILA CLUTCHED the two sides of her dressing gown together as she left the bedroom, and shuffled in her slippers towards the kitchen to make breakfast.

Now me son's out of prison and moved back home he'll bleed me dry of money as usual. I can't stay; especially now Donny's crimes have got more serious. Somehow I'd be involved in his robberies for sure, but where can I go this time, especially now I have Mickey in my life.

Other times she had escaped to her sister's, but Bella now lived in Adelaide...too far away and too expensive to get there. She frowned, knowing that Donny had become a habitual criminal and would soon be hiding from the police again, or back in goal. *It's like he's on a revolving door, and he's putting me on one, round and round and back to the same spot every time he gets out.*

She realised she must think of a plan quickly but nothing readily presented itself.

....

Donny was tossing a shovel into the back of his truck. It clanged loudly then lay still. He flicked back his long black hair, wiped his mud-covered hands on the side of his ragged jeans and stepped over the newly dug mound of loose soil. He swung himself into the truck and revved the engine, startling every bird within metres. He jumped the truck forward, flinging aside any low branches in his path. Pressing down further on the accelerator he continued to bounce his truck through the rough bush track and back on to the road.

In front of the house he screeched the vehicle to a sudden halt.

He jumped out; slamming the door shut behind him the instant his feet hit the ground.

"Have you seen Mickey? He's not around," asked his worried mother as he entered the kitchen.

"Your darling Mickey's left...done a bunk...ain't comin' back." Donny could not keep a look of satisfaction from his face.

"He wouldn't leave." Her voice was strong with conviction. "He adores me and I him. Besides, he's all I've had for company since your father left and you keep getting put in the clink." She noticed a smirk appearing on Donny's face and frowned. "What have you done?" she demanded.

Donny noisily swallowed some cornflakes and looked away.

"WHAT have you done?" Realization of the truth hit her and she flopped into a chair." Then it was a gun I heard going off earlier, not a truck backfiring?" Not expecting an answer she moaned. "I'll miss him."

Donny grimaced. "Yeah. Don't I know it, but I won't. He kept me awake every night roaming around the house, and I needin' me sleep...didn't have much when I was inside." He grimaced as if a new thought had suddenly struck him. "Now I'm out of goal and home for good ya can spend ya money on ya son instead."

Twin tears hit the plate with a flat plop, but born of sturdy stuff, Sheila knew she must get away as soon as possible. It would not be long before he was gone, one way or another, but she knew she could not wait around and possibly be involved for receiving property he had stolen, or worse.

All possible avenues of escape were mentally examined and dismissed, until she thought of old Vincent up the road, also on his own. He was always telling her how lonely he was as his eyes focused on her still trim body.

She took it to be a hint and dismissed it as a silly old man's wishful thinking, but all things considered, he wasn't a bad sort and she knew she could manage him. The outline of a plan began to evolve in her mind.

She quietly padded out on to the front verandah and rang Vincent.

"It's Sheila. Yes I'm fine, but I've been worried about you, wondering how you're managing since your legs got weak and you have to use a walking stick most of the time. It's worried me so much, and I know you've been making enquiries about getting help, so I'd like to be your housekeeper, if that's what you'd like."

Vincent, with excitement evident in his voice said, "That would be great, having you help me out when I need it."

Sheila hesitated for a moment then added, "I was thinking of a live-in position." She did not add that she would go back home when Donny left.

Vincent replied immediately. "It's my lucky day. By the way, I've got a job for you right away. When I drove up that bush track to look for mushrooms this morning early, like I do sometimes, I got up to that paddock where the ground is real soft and always moist. It was real muddy after that heavy rain last night, and you wouldn't believe it. There was this poor dog covered in mud. Looks like he's hurt, but he'll be okay. I was just about to wash him and ring the RSPCA, but you can come and help me clean him up first."

"I'll be right over, and don't ring the RSPCA yet." *Mickey darling, hang in there. This is your lucky day, and mine too.*

She grabbed her car keys from the kitchen table, and not bothering to discard her dressing gown for other clothes quickly drove to Vincent's house.

SHADOW IN THE MIST OF MEMORY

I WATCHED HIM from where I was sitting in the theatre's restaurant, and idly wondered why those creases were about his eyes; why that dejection showing in his sagging shoulders, and that despair in his every movement. I wanted to know him. I had so few close friends. I wished to reach out my hand in comfort, but instead I turned my eyes away. I knew I couldn't say anything to him. I shrugged my shoulders, took up my belongings and slid out of the narrow seat – out of the haunt of artists and musicians. I was soon part of the crowd sweeping past the door.

I hurriedly made my way back to the theatre. I had spent too long away as it was. I had to go over a new song with Harry while his orchestra was still practising. I arrived in time, but my mind kept drifting while I sang. Harry grew impatient. The song was new and difficult but after I reined in my thoughts he was happy with the final result.

That opening night I paid less attention than usual to my dressing. I felt somewhat depressed. I was not satisfied with only singing operetta songs. I yearned for the big stage, acting and singing in the musical theatre, perhaps in comedies.

As I sang my eyes wandered over the gathering of music lovers and I secretly hoped I would see the man from the restaurant, for this was the biggest venue in the City of Sydney. I looked in vain. He was nowhere, but somehow his fine handsome face stood out clearly smudging the sea of faces upturned towards the stage. I thought I would probably never see him again...this face that so attracted me...never find out why he was so depressed...so melancholy.

I noticed Harry in the wings frowning. I was singing without zest, but I had ceased to care. Why should I? I was an excellent singer – all Sydney knew that –but if I could get the opportunity to change direction I would take it.

Shortly after I had retreated to my dressing room after the show there were three knocks on the door. It was Harry's code. I called to him to come in.

He sat beside me as I re-arranged my hair. "What's the matter kiddo – something troubling you?" he enquired kindly.

"No," I answered slowly. I did not, could not, explain my strange desire of the evening to enter the life of a stranger...a man who both interested and fascinated me by my lack of knowledge about him.

"You were very preoccupied this evening. Your singing lacked its usual warmth. You know you are such a great part of the orchestra that if you slow up, the orchestra suffers. Sure it's not something I can help with?"

He was treating me as he treated us all, like his children, and I as his favourite. In a flash my throat closed up and I was close to tears.

Harry took my hand in his. "What's wrong kiddo...man trouble?"

"No," I said. "Just...just...well...I'm just sick of singing; sick of working in the same place; of seeing the same people all the time. Forgive me Harry. I don't mean you. You know that. It's something I can't explain. I have always thought first about myself. Why shouldn't I? But tonight I thought about someone else, worried about someone I didn't even know, because his eyes were so desperately sad. Such things I don't notice normally, so it's confusing me."

As my eyes watered Harry put his hands firmly on my shoulders and held my gaze with his. "I know what it is Dell. You have been working so hard lately, day and night, extra rehearsals and everything. It's too much for anyone. You need a break, a change. I know you're somewhat of a loner. You've always refused to come to after-show parties but tonight Lance McKell is holding one. He's the money behind the show as you know, and wants us to meet Craig Sellway from America who's producing some of his musical comedies here in Sydney. I insist you come along. It'll be good for you. So do up that beautiful face of yours, and I'll be back in ten minutes."

At first I thought I wouldn't go. I hated mixing with a lot of people I did not know and I become bored when watching many of them fawning over others for favours. A mic in my hand, the lighting perfect, together with the hush in the audience as I was about to sing, made me feel alive. Even more so when I pretended I was singing in a musical, which had become somewhat of an obsession.

"Coming?" Harry called from the other side of the closed door.

"Yes, I'm coming."

Harry opened the door as I reached it and stood back to allow me to pass. He had one hand behind his back. "Sweetheart," he said lightly.

I smiled and turned to face him, noticing how old he looked in the half light…how his grey hair showed up. I also noticed how lonely he looked. I wondered in that instant if the orchestra was enough to fill his life, to shut out the loss of his wife and child in a car accident. I felt suddenly overcome with guilt at my earlier thoughts – the desire to desert him if the opportunity came. His arm came from behind his back and he held up a corsage of tiny red roses.

"Oh Harry," I exclaimed, overcome. This was not something one would expect from 'business always' Harry.

"Where did you get them at this late hour?" I asked as I pinned them to my frock.

His eyes were twinkling as he chuckled. "Bert the florist next door is an old mate. He lives on the premises so I went next door, woke him up, and got these for you while you were changing. You look beautiful and sure to impress this musical comedy producer. There may be a chance he could use a light orchestra some time too."

When we arrived, loud music combined with the noise of people together, seemed to be the right companions for the coloured lights flooding the grounds of Lance McKell's large mansion. When the charming Mrs McKell met us at the door Harry introduced me. We were led into a large lounge room where about twenty people were sitting, or standing, drinking and gossiping. The man at the piano stopped playing as we entered, and conversations lulled as they glanced toward us. They waved a greeting to Harry and raised their eyebrows at him; it being the first time he had been accompanied by his singer.

Mr McKell seemed to appear out of nowhere and welcomed us. He was fat, short and jovial and I felt at ease with him immediately. He introduced Craig Sellway, tall, good looking, smooth, with a distinct American drawl that helped to make him stand out from the rest of us. He looked at me, or rather, looked me over, smiling his delight – an obviously genuine delight that made me feel warm inside. He made me feel I wanted to have more of his company.

Before I was swept away by the smiling Mr. McKell, Craig Sellway, slapping his side, said. "Lance, be sure this is where the beautiful lady finishes up tonight…in my company. I'd like Dell to try one of my favourite cocktails. I mix them myself."

We passed from group to group, all with familiar names in the theatrical world. When we walked up towards the final group, two men turned face on. My heart stopped beating for a second for I was looking into the eyes of the man I'd seen in the restaurant.

Mr McKell was saying, as if from a distance, "Meet Kenny Wyland."

I was about to say 'Not THE Kenny Wyland!' He was the talk of the town, and the 'catch' of the theatre world. I had heard a lot about him but as I never read the magazines the other girls drooled over I had not seen his photograph. Why had he been eating alone I wondered, when woman would fight each other to be with him.

Mr McKell was still talking. "Kenny Wyland is the most promising male star I've ever had in any of my shows."

Kenny Wyland's eyes were still sad, even though he was smiling as he said, "Lance always jokes like that, but I'm delighted to meet you. Harry has been raving on about his beautiful, lovely singer for so long we were beginning to think he would never show you off in person to the rest of us. But I can see for myself that even he was understating your beauty. I'm sorry I haven't been to any of Harry's recitals as yet, but now I will."

He turned to Harry. "Perhaps you can persuade Dell to sing for us later. Would you mind Miss Cass?"

I hesitated. I was still watching his expressions carefully and wished everyone would disappear, and we'd be alone together. Instead I said "No I wouldn't mind." Later I was annoyed at myself to think I had let myself become weak and ready to agree to whatever he asked.

Lance McKell took us back to Craig Sellway who handed me a cocktail. It was delicious. I listened to him talk about his work and I talked back to him about myself. As I had guessed, you could talk to him and later be surprised at how much you had told him in a short time. He complimented me whenever the opportunity arose, and I smiled shyly at him, as I knew I was expected to. It was as though his flattery was the only thing that meant anything to me. But, at the same time I was listening for sounds of Kenny's voice, hoping he would come closer. But gradually, under the flattering attention of Craig Sellway, Kenny Wyland seemed to drift further and further away. Perhaps it was partly due to the cocktails Craig kept mixing for me.

Harry came over to me to ask me if I was ready to sing. He squeezed my hand as he spoke. That meant 'say yes'.

"I'd love to," was the only reply I could make. Holding my hand he led me to the grand piano and announced my song. As I sang I carefully watched the faces, mainly Kenny Wyland's and Craig Sellway's. It was obvious Craig was impressed. I saw him seemingly asking questions of Harry. Harry had a wide satisfied smile on his face, and knew I was set for stage work if I wanted it. If so, I hoped Harry would be somehow included. Kenny also had appeared impressed but I could not tell whether it was merely surprise at my voice.

When I finished everyone demanded more. I waited for a clue from Harry. He shook his head very slightly and came over to me, stood beside me, and announced. "Terribly sorry, but Dell has been singing earlier tonight and I know you will forgive me if I have to look after my star singer." Harry certainly knew what he was doing.

We went back to Craig, who complimented me and then left to mix more cocktails of his own liking. I knew he would also make one for me.

Kenny walked over to us as Harry turned to chat with someone. Kenny and I were as alone as we could be at that moment. I noticed how tall he was and that there was red in his hair as the light caught it. He wasn't smiling as his sad eyes gazed quietly down at me. "Congratulations and thanks Miss Cass. May I call you Dell?"

My heart missed a beat. "Of course."

"And you call me Kenny. Everyone else does. He was smiling now. "Your singing is delightful. I'd like to come and hear you sing tomorrow evening. Our show finished today. I have two weeks off before I start rehearsals for the new show, so I'm free for a bit. If I get a seat up close to the front I'll watch your beautiful expressive blue eyes as you sing. Do you think you could spare me a look, even a quick one, if I manage to get a ticket?"

I wanted to say, 'If you're there you'll be the only person I will see whether I look at you or not.' Instead I said, "I might even look at you twice Mr Wyland...that is if I remember."

Neither of us noticed Craig coming up to us. "A special drink for you Del," he interrupted. "Oh, I'm sorry. Am I intruding?" Looking directly at me he continued. "Kenny seems to have turned out to be my rival for your attention this evening...but then, looking at you Dell no man could resist you."

"Must circulate." Kenny excused himself and the conversation around me went on. I rather liked it, as I didn't have to listen very carefully. They were all talking about my singing, flattering me, and I can take a lot of flattery. I secretly held on to the thought that Kenny would be at the theatre the next evening.

When everyone began to leave Craig said, "Johnny McKell has kindly put a car at my disposal while I'm here, so may I have the honour of escorting you home?"

For a moment I did not answer or look at him. I was glancing around the room. I could see Kenny helping a blonde girl on with her coat.

Craig misunderstood my motive. He said, "Harry's in the kitchen Dell. I'll fetch him for you. Excuse me." He hurried off.

The blonde walked past with Kenny walking behind her. He stopped when in line with me and he bent his face down to mine and whispered, "Those beautiful roses are part of you...I love roses and white camellias. Camellias would match your soft white skin. Do you like them?"

"They're one of my favourites too." I replied quickly. Although I knew that Kenny, like many others in the field, would be an expert at flattery, in my heart, I hoped he meant what he said. The blonde had turned back no doubt wondering where he was.

"Goodnight Dell," he said as Harry came up.

I told him about Craig's invitation to give me a ride home and he asked in an undertone. "Are you sure you want to? You only met him tonight."

"Of course I do. Isn't he a celebrity in the same music business at you?" I spoke louder than normal hoping Kenny, putting on his coat at the door, heard me.

Craig returned and we both farewelled Harry and everyone else close by as we left the house.

Outside I saw Kenny seated at the wheel of a small sports car. The blonde was beside him. I slipped my arm through Craig's who clasped it firmly. I was satisfied.

Craig drove me home via the harbour front. Then he pulled up and with a full moon overhead we silently watched reflected city lights being smashed into millions of tiny dancing stars by the restless water.

Craig slipped his arm around me. I laid my head on his shoulder. It was comfortable and peaceful here with him. Neither of us spoke as we watched the scene before us. Then he stirred, straightened and putting his hand under my chin tilted my face so he could look directly into my eyes. "Along with everything else I've said to you I have to add that you're cute."

I cuddled up closer as a way of saying 'thanks'. I studied his finely cut features, his perfectly shaped lips, and the humour around his eyes. As with all successful men he had about him an atmosphere of success and luxury. As he moved closer the atmosphere overcame me and I felt this was what I needed: a man who could open the door to everything I wanted. He drew me closer and kissed me. He knew how to send thrills through a woman.

I suddenly thought of the roses I wore. I felt them. They were a mass of crushed red petals. As I unpinned them I could hear in my mind Kenny's voice saying, 'those beautiful roses are perfect for you. I love them.' My rising desire for Craig had suddenly disappeared.

"Sorry I crushed your flowers Dell, but I'll buy you more, millions more if you wish...in fact all the roses in the world."

"That's very nice Craig, but what I want now is to go home. I'm very tired."

"Sorry I've been very selfish, but you are irresistible."

I said nothing as he settled back in his seat and started the car.

After a tight hug and a lingering kiss at my door, he was understanding enough not to expect me to invite him inside. As he was going he said, "I'll be going north for a few weeks. If you'd like us to get together again I'll ring and let you know when I'm arriving back."

"Of course I want to see you again." He kissed me quickly and left.

The next evening I had just completed dressing in my favourite black velvet. It makes my eyes look darker. It also shows up my white arms; my white shoulders and emphasised the dark auburn streaked through my dark hair. As I was putting the finishing touches to my make-up a knock came on the dressing room door.

"Come in." The knock continued. Irritated I opened it. The delivery boy was standing there holding a small box. I took it and gave him a tip. I wondered if it was from Harry. If it was, why send it with the boy? I opened it quickly. Inside was a perfectly white camellia with tiny green leaves surrounding it. The note attached read. 'Don't forget to look my way.......Kenny.'

I took out the spray and held the camellia close to my cheek for a moment, then clasped it into the curls haloing my face. I looked at my reflection in the mirror and was satisfied.

I walked slowly out on to the stage as Harry was announcing me. I felt radiant and must have looked it as I waited for the clapping to subside. I kept looking straight ahead. I had made enquiries and knew where Kenny was sitting. I hoped he liked me wearing his camellia.

That night I put everything I could into my singing and saw Harry was delighted. I wanted so much to look at Kenny but concentrated on looking everywhere else, even straight ahead as I walked off the stage.

On returning to my dressing room I was confronted by Kenny. I was delighted but momentarily thrown off balance. He was leaning back in the spare chair facing me. His arm hung over the side, and his long legs stretched out before him, as if it were his dressing room, not mine. There was a twinkle in his eye that showed he was enjoying himself at my expense.

I fell in with the charade, saying nothing as I walked over to my dressing table. I sat down as if I had scarcely noticed him, although all the time a ripple of excitement ran through me, and it was all I could do to keep from smiling with delight.

He watched me pick up my comb, watched me run it slowly and carefully through the front of my hair with forced carelessness. I felt his eyes on me, amused, analytic. The pose became a strain. I felt I had to talk, hating the fact that I was the first to give in.

"Well, it's Kenny. What a surprise."

"Dell you were great, both on stage... and now." We both turned to face each other at the same moment, and laughed. "But you didn't look at me, not once." His tone had become reproachful. "You forgot, didn't you?"

"No I didn't"

"Then why did you admire every other man in the place except me?"

I turned my head away, my eyes away from his eyes. I was trying to think of something to say that would not give away my feelings for him, when he rose, moved towards me and put his hand over mine. It was a warm, gentle caress, and I felt a desire for him to keep it there, but instead I pulled it away and said lightly. "Can't have it. I might need it." The tension was gone.

"I really came here to ask if I could escort you home, or out for coffee...whatever. You're finished for the night aren't you?"

"I might think about it, then I might say 'yes.' I have to change so wait outside!" He grinned and left.

I felt very light inside as I joined Kenny. My days of depression had lifted.

He drove towards the Harbour, to the same area as Craig had after the party. "Would Your Highness like to view the waterways of Sydney's version of Vienna?"

"Yes, but not here." I was thinking of Craig. "Go further along where we can see the bridge."

He turned the car and drove further along. He parked it close to a large weeping willow with its drooping branches breaking the surface of the water. We watched as the full moon made the bridge look part of a distant fairyland. As I settled back I felt everything was complete. I was with Kenny. I turned to face him. The breeze ruffled his hair and I imagined the red in it, hidden now in the half-light. His face looked boyish but the sad look had returned. I had a wild instinct to put my arms around him and hold him close to me, as it was the same look that had drawn me to him in the restaurant.

"Is Your Highness comfortable?"

"No, slave."

"Good. That'll soon be rectified." He slipped his arm about my shoulders and pressed his face against mine. "The camellia suited your outfit tonight, and you looked a picture in that black velvet." He hesitated for a moment then turned and gently kissed me. "Why do I like you?" he whispered.

"I don't know." I couldn't tell him what I was feeling...not yet.

He looked across at the water and spoke quietly. "When I was very little my father brought me to town and the lights on the water fascinated me, so that afterwards I would ask my father to bring me home some of the lights I'd seen in the water. It took a long time to realise that you can't hold them. They're beautiful but unattainable, like a lot of things in life." He was silent for a moment then added, "I'm getting too serious Your Highness."

"Did you always want to act?" I asked. It seemed somehow necessary for me to change the subject and it was all I could think of to say.

"Yes, my mother was an actress. Her stage successes were my first bedtime stories. Anyway we're talking too much about K.W. What about you Dell? Did you always sing?"

"No, except in the bath. I never really thought I could sing well until I met Harry. I was nineteen when I visited the city and heard music I really liked. It was an orchestra practicing. I listened and started to sing right there in the street, in front of that building. No one was around, but then a man came out. He asked me to come inside and sing for him. It was Harry. I never had so much fun. Harry talked me into taking lessons so I could sing with the orchestra. Now it's the most popular in Sydney."

"I agree there, and his singer Dell Cass is the dream sweetheart of every man who hears her sing."

I lowered my eyes and said. "Oh..." I knew I was supposed to be coy, but was secretly pleased he knew how popular I was.

"It's getting late. I'm on again tomorrow night," I said.

He ignored my hint. "Dell, I know of a little café open twenty-four hours. Like some coffee and whatever?"

I had a lot of fun that night. Kenny was everything I had dreamed about in a man, but no matter how I tried, Kenny always steered the conversation away from his personal life.

I joined him every night after the show, and Craig seemed to be part of another age and the party seemed years past. My thoughts only revolved around Kenny. We spent all our free days...heavenly days...together.

A call came from Craig to say he would be returning the next day. I shrugged and thought, 'So be it.'

That night became our last night together. We sat by the ocean watching the moonlit sea rolling in to the beach. It was soothing and restful. Kenny was very quiet, quieter than he had ever been with me. Then he surprised me by asking, "Do you love me?"

"I think so," I said offhandedly not wanting to feel too vulnerable.

"I find myself in love with you Dell." With utter joy and a heart ready to burst with happiness I tried to draw him closer, but he drew back and said softly, "No Dell…don't make it harder for me…and you. I've got to tell you something that has been driving me crazy."

I mentally braced myself. I wanted to shout, 'No, don't tell me. Don't tell me anything that will spoil this beautiful thing we have together.' But I closed my eyes and said, "Go on."

"It's hard." He hesitated. "But I'll start at the beginning. I met Fay when I was starting my acting career. She was frail and delicate, and dependent. Within a few months we married." He paused, and life seem to ebb from my body as the words made wounds deeper than a knife.

"I think it was her frailness that made me want to protect her, but the marriage only lasted a year. I think the strain of travel and little money – I was only starting off my career then – were too much for her. She was diagnosed with advanced breast cancer. Her family had spoilt her and so did I at first, but when I had no money left she went back to her parents. Two days ago she wrote and said her mother had passed away and she wanted to come back to me."

I pictured a little white-faced, helpless creature…a little butterfly deciding to come back to the garden, seeing it was flowering again. I looked at Kenny and thought bitterly. 'You weak fool,' as hate and bitterness made me want to run and hide. With a firm hold on my emotions, I managed to say, "So you have decided to take her back; give it another try."

He ignored or didn't see the undercurrent in my tone for he went on. "She hasn't long to live, you know."

In my disappointment I wanted to say, 'She'll live longer than you I guarantee. I know her type.'

"Dell, you know I love you…only you."

I sighed. 'If he knew how much I loved him he would never go back to…to her, but I was too frightened to tell him.'

"I won't go back if you don't want me too," he said.

I knew he was putting the responsibility for his own decisions on to me. I felt he wanted assurance on whichever course he was to take. I had a sudden vision of the adverse publicity I would get if I stopped him and she went to the press.

"Am I right to take her back?" He was earnest, pathetic, pleading with me to understand his position.

"Take her back if you think that's the right thing to do." I was surprised to hear myself say, and proud of how I controlled the tone, as I could have spat the words out.

"Dell darling, how can I thank you? I'll never forget you and I'll make it up to you someday I swear."

"Take me home."

He started the car without another word.

Inside my unit I flung myself on the bed. I knew that when Harry called for me in the morning he would see what state I was in and be aghast, but I needn't have worried. He sat beside me and put his arm around me. "Kenny isn't it?"

"Yes." Between sniffling I told him everything

"I know kiddo," Harry said kindly. "I lost ones I loved too. Look, do you know Craig is due here midday?"

"Yes, but I don't want to see him."

"Yes you do...my orders. You take tonight and tomorrow off. I'll get Marie to fill in for you. Go off with Craig and try not to think about Kenny. You're young. You mustn't be troubled for too long by life's setbacks."

"Thanks Harry. You're so kind. I wish you knew how grateful I feel."

Harry squeezed my arm as he said, 'bye' kiddo.'

At noon Craig arrived. I forced a welcoming smile as he entered. I had already let him know I was having the day off. He thought it was especially for him.

Craig's company was invigorating. He lived a fast life and I spent a lot of time with him. It made me forget the sad eyes...the hair with the red in it.

Weeks passed. I heard from friends that Kenny's wife was becoming well known as she was constantly at the theatre where Kenny was acting in a play. It had caused quite a stir when the news was publicised, as Kenny had never given any indication that he was married, and now he was painted as the ideal husband.

'She's a little hypocrite. She doesn't love him,' was my reaction.

I was nicer to Craig than I thought it would be possible for me to be under the circumstances, and he loved it. He was easy to work with, and I was soon rehearsing for the lead in his next musical play. Harry said I had changed and didn't like it. He said I had become cold, too cold, although if time allowed I could still sing with his orchestra.

After a very successful opening night Craig proposed. I was on the threshold of my life. I was about to realise everything I ever wanted, and Craig could help me reach the top, so naturally I accepted. I was also genuinely fond of him, although love did not come into it. At the same time the publicity was widespread and was good for both of us. When I finally reached my dressing room I found a box. Inside was a single white camellia. A note said, "Dell, you were magnificent...congratulations...Love Kenny.

Craig entered, and I put the box down. "Who's that from?"

"Oh," I said and shrugged. "Just Kenny Wyland. He liked the show."

"Of course...everyone did, but we have to hurry, the McKells are waiting."

"Are you wearing the camellia?" he asked.

"No darling." I drew closer to him. "I refuse to wear flowers from anyone but my fiancée." He was delighted and kissed me quickly on both cheeks.

We were the last to arrive and immediately the centre of attention. Even Harry was being showered with compliments about my performance, and I let everyone know that he gave me my first singing lessons.

When most of the people drifted around the room I realised Kenny was present. I had been so wrapped up with the reactions to my success, and my engagement, that I had not thought of the possibility of him being there. I held back the desire to talk to him. I noticed he looked sadder, older, and wasn't smiling. Beside him was a tiny blonde, pretty and frail.

'Too frail looking,' I thought angrily, and then felt miserably depressed. But I forced a gaiety, which I only kept up by continually drinking Craig's cocktails.

When people were congratulating us on our engagement I saw the pain in Kenny's eyes and felt strangely satisfied to think I had hurt him as he had hurt me.

A month later Craig and I were married. I cried when I accepted his ring. I told Craig it was for joy. Four weeks later we left for America. He said he had been too long away from his company headquarters. I persuaded Craig to include Harry and his orchestra into his plans. He compromised by asking Harry and half the orchestra to join his company, as he said he had some 'good boys back home' he had to include.

During all the excitement of the voyage and the new surroundings, I began to think I was in love with Craig at last, but after we settled I realised it wasn't love...not the love I felt for Kenny. I also found that Craig was only concerned about how I looked to others. Craig had obtained what Americans called 'a trophy wife', and to them this one had an 'amusing' accent. In a strange way it was easy for me as I learned how to act to please everyone.

At the beginning of our marriage I would close my eyes and imagine Craig's arms around me were Kenny's, but after a while Craig himself drifted emotionally away from me, and I was not interested enough to find out why.

Then Carmel Ann was born, and Craig's love and mine for her brought us closer than we had ever been. She was radiantly beautiful, and had the delicate quality of an angel. We were still in New York, and Harry was Carmel Ann's godfather, but acted like a proud grandfather. Then Craig decided to go to South America for a year.

Harry wanted to buy a small nightclub and stay in New York so we sadly parted, and I missed him dreadfully. When we moved to South America we hired a young nanny.

On the opening night of our new show Carmel Ann was a

little off-colour. We gave strict instructions to the nanny to get a doctor straight away if Carmel Ann's mild condition changed, and to contact us immediately. We heard nothing from her.

When we arrived home happy and joyful after midnight, Carmel Ann had a high temperature. We immediately dismissed the nanny and frantically called the doctor. She had a severe case of pneumonia. A week later, she passed away. Perhaps if Harry had been with us we would not have lost her, because when Craig and I could not take Carmel Ann with us anywhere Harry would care for her as lovingly as a grandfather would.

Craig and I, heartbroken and distraught, became guilt tormented and a wider distance grew between us. It became so strained that we could not continue living any kind of peaceful life together. Everywhere we went we had to dodge people who insisted on extending sympathies. I could not cope with that, nor with the media people who followed us everywhere. It was then I decided to drop out of Craig's shows. This was not hard to do for all my ambitions had died with Carmel Ann. Craig was forced to agree. Through strain and shattered nerves I had become drawn and looked ten years older. I was no longer his 'trophy wife.'

It was almost a relief when Craig became infatuated with a beautiful South American girl and acted besotted with her, and left me in solitude to grieve.

Harry kept urging me to give it time, but a future with Craig was now impossible. Harry would welcome me I knew, so I informed Craig I was leaving for New York. We talked almost casually over everything and decided to divorce. Or rather Craig decided on the divorce. I think he hated the tension between us as much as I did. As far as I was concerned it didn't matter whether we stayed married or not, but it did to Craig and to his South American girlfriend.

Harry was overjoyed when I told him I was coming to see him. I left South America, disinterested in life, disinterested in everything. At that moment I did not even care whether or not I saw Harry, but he was the only genuine friend I had – the only friend who would understand.

I finally arrived in New York. The city no longer thrilled me as it once did. At the airport an obviously excited Harry rushed up eagerly when he saw me, taking me in his arms before everyone, like a doting father.

At his unit, after I had settled my belongings into the spare bedroom, he led me gently to the lounge. We sat close together and he put her arm around me. I put my head on his shoulder and cried. I had been so tightly knotted inside since Carmel Ann's sudden death tears would not come. Now they would not stop. I blurted out everything as I had always done with him and I gradually began to feel a great deal of relief.

In the weeks that followed, I settled into a routine with Harry. I accompanied him to his restaurant and to the theatre where his orchestra played on a Saturday night. I began to get interested in singing again.

A week later, as we were seated around the dining table, he said, "I saw you smile today for the first time since you came here."

"Probably because I'm now sleeping throughout the night without being drugged to the eyeballs. I love going out with you during the day. I am even starting to look to the future. I am so grateful for all you've done for me."

"Forget it, but now you're better, or almost, I have something to tell you. I am now the proud owner of a little cottage on the outskirts of New York. It's a peaceful little place...ideal for a rest. In fact I think you should spend time there and work out what you want to do with your life. You may want to go back to Sydney or perhaps join me in my endeavours. It's up to you." We began to talk about home and both felt a little homesick.

"We'll take a trip back home sometime, eh Dell?"

"That would be great," I replied though I thought it was probably a long way off.

On the weekend following, Harry drove me to his cottage. I clapped my hands in rapture at seeing the white and green painted cottage. It seemed to me to have been copied from a children's fairy book. The house with its gabled roof and old-fashioned brick base and heavy wooden door seemed unreal.

"As you know I have to get back for rehearsals, but there's a maid who'll open the door and let you in."

Harry carried my luggage to the door of the house, as I was still gazing, wrapped in the scene before me. As he turned to move back to his car I gave him a quick kiss on the cheek. 'Thanks Harry," I said sincerely.

Entering through the squeaking gate I heard Harry call back. "Get Angela to help with the bags. The bedrooms are upstairs. Pick whichever one you like. I'll ring you tomorrow."

"Okay, 'bye."

Inside was the type of cosy, country style house I had lived in as a child. It had made me feel safe, comfortable, and on rainy days warm and secure. 'Harry knows me so well,' I thought.

A young girl in a black dress and white cap came up to greet me, while the smell of chicken being roasted made me feel hungry.

"Hello." I smiled at her.

"Welcome Madam. Do you want to see the bedrooms first?"

"Not yet. I'd like to explore down here first."

"There's a terrace with a nice garden at the back, Mrs. Sellway."

I wandered through glass doors on to a patio with potted plants and a background of flowering trees. I noticed the back of a man relaxing on a garden bench further down. There was red in his hair. I caught my breath. 'Kenny?' I whispered, but my mind said 'impossible, he's in Australia.'

The man turned. "Dell? Oh Dell, I've been waiting for you."

Was I dreaming? No, it was Kenny. He looked older. His face was lined but still striking. He sprang forward, took my arm and led me to one of the wooden benches. I sat down helplessly, telling myself that I must be dreaming.

"Didn't Harry tell you I was here?"

I shook my head.

"No wonder you look so surprised, but I've been over here for a few months. I was invited over by the New York Players Association. I've been writing and producing my own plays for eight years now. Of course the first one I came to see was Harry. I knew he would be able to tell me how you were and where."

"Did your wife come too?" I had to ask.

"She passed away four months after you married Craig."

My hopes soared, but I made no comment. "How did you know where he was?"

"I guess he didn't tell you that either, but we've been corresponding ever since he came over. It was the only way I could find out how you were, and if you were happy. In fact, he was the one who persuaded me to come to New York."

"So you know...?"

"Yes, and I'm sorry...very sorry." His voice was soft and full of understanding. Then he added, "Perhaps I can make you laugh with my more humorous plays. But what about you? How long are you staying here Dell?"

"Harry said I was to stay until I feel like moving."

"Harry told me the same thing."

"That means...?"

They both laughed with understanding of Harry's tactics.

Kenny bowed. "Would Your Highness like a tour of the garden before the maid calls us for tea?"

"Excellent suggestion My Lord."

With their arms tightly wrapped around each other's waists, they walked along the path to stop between the overhanging branches of the ornamental trees, where they hungrily kissed.

HIS LAST GOOD DEED

ON A SHOWERY, WINDY, WINTER'S DAY, a small group of mourners, all clad in long grey coats, stood cold and miserable on rain-soaked sticky mud beside Clarence's open grave. It took a strong sense of loyalty to a fellow church member and old friend to be there at all, bidding 'Reverend' Clarence Dudley a final farewell. Meanwhile unknown to them Clarence, the 'Reverend' now in spirit watched them from above.

"Poor old Clarence." said one mourner placing flowers on the coffin. "Never had a chance at happiness, with that bully of a father of his. Nothing Clarence did pleased his old man. Always being punished for something he was, poor kid. Since his father died, he's been stuck in that house all alone with his Bible. No wonder he got the nickname 'Reverend.' I don't think he ate much. All skin and bone he was."

Clarence, although no longer in the flesh, nodded in agreement.

"He never talked to anyone after service, just raced home to read that Bible of his. He let the farm go to rack and ruin too," added another.

"Yep. All that extra praying and strict discipline is what done it. He didn't need it. Why, he wouldn't hurt a fly. I remember when his old man once caught him talking to some girls. Well, you never...."

"Shush! Look! Pastor's nearly finished."

"Hope he's quick. I'm cold and wet."

The Pastor scattered earth on to the coffin and the mourners began to dribble away.

Clarence still hovered over the scene, and an unexplainable sadness overwhelmed him. Poised between earth, heaven, or perhaps hell, after a life, he was told and believed, was of continual failure, he wondered where he would go. His father continually foretold hell for him. His days were worsened by breath-denying asthma attacks, which strangely disappeared after his father died. 'Those attacks are punishment for your sins, boy,' his father would say. Clarence was not sure what his 'sins' were, but accepted his father's declaration that, as a father he was always right. *How proud father would've been if he'd lived to see me in these last years; all spent atoning for my 'sins'.*

The grip of sadness was suddenly replaced by a feeling of peace. But no sooner had it begun when it dispersed, for his mind refused to let go of his past. 'Keep all your thoughts on the Lord, so no sinful, lustful thoughts can enter.' These were his father's instructions when he became aware of girls, and particularly after he met Kathleen, beautiful Kathleen O'Day.

As always Clarence took his father's advice seriously, but desire for his one and only love remained stubbornly set, ever ready to intrude into his praying. Her face swam before him. He pictured Kathleen with her long dark wavy hair flying in the wind, her rippling laugh, and her green eyes soft with love for him.

Love, happiness, and despair closely followed one another after his father realised Clarence was in love. He forbade him to see Kathleen. 'She's not one of us,' his father would say. He would hold prayer meetings to counteract his son's 'sinful' desires. Kathleen was also forbidden to see Clarence. A year later broken-hearted delicate Kathleen became sick and before the year was out suddenly died.

Clarence winced as he re-lived those nightmare days of thirty years ago, filled with a grief that the hard work and prayers his father prescribed could not dispel. Broken in spirit and health he became the puppet of his father. After his father's death Clarence developed a lean, frail appearance. The skin stretched transparent over the high cheekbones of his pale face, and his eyes were sunken like dark pools. He studied the Bible until late into the night. Had he atoned for his transgressions? He was not sure and it worried him.

He drew his mind back to relive that snippet of peace he had felt seconds before, when his mind had become blank and drifted into nothingness. As he tried, a mountain of mist rose engulfing him. It then quickly receded to reveal two ghostly white transparent figures. They gently and firmly took his arms, guiding him into what to Clarence was a thick cloud. He sucked in his breath as it dispersed to reveal a glistening golden gate, which opened wide as they floated closer.

A building tall and white confronted the amazed Clarence. A large glowing open doorway edged with lights seemed to beckon them to enter. Once inside they drifted through chambers and down corridors, until they reached a large room, the ceiling of which disappeared, then reappeared, while the walls changed colour continuously.

"What is this place?" queried Clarence. "It doesn't look like the heaven or hell my father told me about." His companions smiled but did not answer.

He became aware of a large glass-like table, tinted blue, and a man in a white robe seated behind it. Clarence's escorts stopped, bowed, and the figure behind the table nodded.

He looked at Clarence. "Welcome...err...name?" he asked

"Clarence." was the whispered reply.

"Other name?"

Clarence cleared his throat. "Dudley."

"Welcome. Angela, where are you? Would you give me his records please? I cannot be expected to remember everything."

Angela, beautiful beyond Clarence's comprehension, floated into view as if cloaked in soft white light. She handed over a silver sheet.

"This isn't Heaven is it?" enquired a dazed Clarence. One of his companions whispered, "No, it is not. This is the foyer. He is a Guardian. You must get the okay from him before you can be admitted. It would be too much of a shock if you were suddenly transported from one existence to another."

"Hmmm." The Guardian was examining the silver sheet while Clarence quivered with worry and apprehension. He then raised his head, looking directly at Clarence. "I am sorry but you do not quite make Heaven and you are too good for Hell. But, I think we should give you another chance...you know...to edge over into Heaven. You will return to earth for one week and carry out one last good deed. Next Saturday night at midnight you will return and I will look into your case again. Your escorts will go with you to help, without interfering of course. Next please." Clarence and his escorts stepped back into a rising mist that blinded Clarence. He closed his eyes.

Feeling cool air fanning his face he opened his eyes to find himself in town. He was standing in front of the City Hall that he had not seen since childhood. Buses followed buses with loud nerve-racking grappling brakes. Cars roared their motors and paperboys selling newspapers shouted for attention. It was all very jarring on Clarence's nerves, accustomed as he was to the quietness of the farm. A woman hurrying by bumped into him. Quickly he seated himself on one of the bus stop benches. *Oh, my. What can I do now?* Hopelessness was now close to taking over his mind.

A young man who had been sitting next to him moved away, leaving his newspaper on the seat. Clarence picked it up and handled it gingerly. 'Newspapers are the voice of the evil one,' he could hear his father say. 'But father,' he mentally argued. 'Perhaps it can be used for good. If I can find something good to do for someone, I'll be able to join you in Heaven.'

He opened the paper and scanned its pages. He could not find any 'Good Deeds Wanted Done' heading anywhere. In disappointment he cast the paper aside. Then he recalled the many children the Pastor's wife had comforted. *Perhaps I could find a lost child and restore it to its mother like she's done, or maybe help an elderly lady cross the street.* He felt satisfied with his reasoning and looked expectantly around, but he could not see any lost child or any feeble old lady needing assistance. "Oh my," wailed Clarence.

The day began to slip away and the traffic rose to a higher peak of noise and impatience. The City Hall clock boomed out five loud chimes. Crowds began to spill from shops and offices to mill around Clarence, before they hurried away to board their public transport. Then the city gradually slowed its pace and the street-lights flickered on, one by one.

'What will I do now?' he asked himself for what seemed the hundredth time but it remained unanswered, for life had not taught Clarence to make decisions.

A plump middle-aged woman seated herself beside

Clarence. She looked him up and down, and then began chatting. "Good to get off me feet. Done nothin' but rush all day. I'm lookin' for a job and I've been everywhere. Say, can I borrow ya paper for a bit? There might be somethin' I missed."

Clarence nervously looked into the untidy woman's smiling face and stammered. "Well...It's not mine. Someone left, and..."

"Ah! Down on ya luck is ya...ya poor love?" She looked at him sympathetically, and continued. "I think I saw ya here when I passed hours ago. Ain't ya got a home to go to, or has the missus throwed ya out?"

"Oh no, I'm not married." Clarence quickly blanketed out any assumption of that sort. "I just have to find somewhere to stay and I don't know the city very well."

"Ahhh." Again she oozed sympathy. "I thought ya looked lost. Why I wouldn't invite just anyone, but ya look a decent bloke, so ya can come to my place. Me eldest son Donny's away at present for a brief stay as a guest of royalty ya might say. Ya can use his room. Have ya got any money?" Then, quickly before he could reply, she went on. "If ya ain't, ya can still stay 'till ya get a job. Ya lookin' for a job ain't ya?"

"A job? Yes, I suppose I am," replied Clarence, thinking this could be the answer to his problem. He would surely meet someone at a job for whom he could do a good deed, although he had no idea what he would be capable of doing.

"Well, if ya comin' come, 'cos here's me bus." She shuffled off. Clarence rose and followed her. When boarding the bus the driver waited for Clarence to pay the fare. Clarence automatically put his hand into his pocket. To his surprise he felt money and drew out more than enough to pay the fares. Clarence glanced up towards Heaven and muttered, "Thanks."

The woman was still chattering. "...and me name's Ferna Fletcher. Call me Ferna and I'll call ya?"

"Oh...Clarence... Clarence Dudley."

"Okay Clarie."

The journey was short. After alighting they entered a narrow street, Ferna led Clarence up the steps of one of the many dilapidated houses, and into a long dingy hall. Ferna switched on the lights. He was taken aback to see expensive solid wood furniture, and ornaments that expressed unexpected good taste.

Ferna saw him staring. "Like 'em do ya?"

"Yes," replied Clarence, embarrassed.

"Presents from me son. When Bill or Donny take a fancy to somethin' they just have to get it for their mum," she replied proudly.

She paused before an open door and entered the room. "This here's ya room. Ain't ya got no clothes? No bag anywhere stashed?"

"I...left in a hurry."

"I understand. Ya didn't pay ya bill. It happens to all of us lovey."

He looked into the room and shuddered. He was nervous of strangers, fearful of strange houses, and as for other people's beds! Trying to stay calm, he told himself that if the opportunity to do a good deed came quickly he would soon be gone.

Ferna pulled open a drawer and handed him a pair of pajamas. They were too large and too gaudy but he reluctantly accepted them.

"Ya can buy some clothes tomorrah," she said as she left him.

Clarence, frightened Ferna might come back, quickly changed and climbed into bed. He wanted to stay awake in case she did, but his eyes grew heavy. He was only asleep for a short time when he was awakened by male voices arguing, and to Clarence's horror they sounded intoxicated. Their raised slurred voices, the clinking of glasses, and the slamming of bottles on to a table went on for hours.

Clarence stayed awake, fearing he would be attacked, perhaps murdered. He knew such things happened in big cities. Then he wondered whether he could be killed, as he was already dead. Too tired to continue this line of thought, he fell into a fitful sleep.

Ferna's rasping voice calling him for breakfast woke Clarence. He felt groggy but he was determined to get his good deed over quickly, if he could find one to do, and then be on his way.

In the kitchen Clarence was surprised to discover that, in contrast to the up-market items in the rest of the house, he was forced to sit on a slightly rickety chair and a table so obviously well used, Clarence wondered why it had not been replaced years ago.

They ate off its bare surface from everything in its original tin or bottle. Ferna used her fingers to stuff food into her mouth. She spoke with a mouthful of food. "Sorry about the noise last night, but me other son Bill and 'is mate worked 'til late. They get a bit excited sometimes but they're good lads. They're catchin' up on a bit of shut-eye now."

Clarence merely nodded. He went on to finish his slice of toast and drink his glass of water – having refused Ferna's offer of a cup of tea or beer.

Suddenly Ferna dragged her chair closer to Clarence and announced. "There's a beaut job goin' at Ascot, but it's for two. How about that? Look, a husband and wife wanted, gardener and housekeeper...a live-in job."

"I beg your pardon," interrupted Clarence, rising from his chair. "Husband and wife indeed. What are you suggesting?"

Grabbing his sleeve she jerked him back on to his chair. "Ahh, keep ya shirt on," she patiently asserted. "I don't mean we'd be husband and wife. We'll be brother and widda sister. I need ya and ya need me. It should be apples."

"Apples?"

"Goodo!"

Clarence's lips compressed into a thin line. "I do not tell lies and..."

"That's okay by me if ya wanta be a goody goody. I'll tell the lies."

"But I really couldn't think of..."

"Please," she interrupted him, with a pleading tone in her voice. "Ya'd be doin' a poor woman a good turn." She wiped away imaginary tears with a grubby tissue.

Good turn! Clarence suddenly remembered why he was

there.

"Well, perhaps it'll be all right," he agreed slowly, thinking, 'This could be what I'm looking for. I'd be doing Ferna a good deed.'

"You'll need some clothes. Have ya got enough dough on ya?"

"I think so." He did not want to check his pockets in front of her.

"Well we have to get ya some clothes if we're goin' for this job. So come on then." She rose, ignoring the need to clean up. Clarence trailed behind.

At the shops, Ferna tried to persuade Clarence to buy a suit but to no avail. The voice of his economizing nature kept whispering to him. *'Buy a suit for only one week, certainly not!*' "Trousers, shirts, and a cardigan will do," he said firmly as she ushered him into the change room.

The next purchases were shoes, which she forced him to change into. After choosing his other necessary personal items Ferna, ready to leave, successfully concealed her impatience when Clarence spent a considerable amount of time searching for a Bible, which he joyfully purchased.

Ferna then guided Clarence, clinging to their parcels, to another bus stop to take them to their prospective employer's home. "We'll go there now. It's still early…before anyone else gets there." They did not have long to wait.

Thirty minutes later they had reached the home of Mrs. Stafford-Jones. She interviewed them in the sunken lounge of her architect-designed brick home, set in a large rambling garden. Clarence stammered his name when asked and was grateful when Ferna took over the conversation. But he was astounded to hear her tell the most outrageous lies about their relationship and previous employment. He turned his attention away, and stared at a spot high on the wall and prayed for her soul. Then a happy Ferna nudged him, nodded, and he knew they had been employed.

Mrs. Stafford-Jones took Ferna to the housekeeper's room beneath her high house. She then showed Clarence his room, which was attached to the garage outside. Once inside alone he began to have strong misgivings. He had agreed to the deception because he believed he was doing Ferna a good turn. He now felt that being party to her lies would surely cancel out his original good intention. Confused, and feeling that any likelihood of gaining heaven was now lost, he opened his Bible to seek comfort.

As each day crept by, Clarence despaired of finding the 'right good deed' to perform. He was becoming desperate. No opportunities had thrown themselves at him. The final day of his allotted time arrived. Clarence hovered nervously in the kitchen while Ferna ignored him and kept ironing. The Stafford-Joneses were attending the Governor's Ball that night and most of Ferna's day was being spent helping Mrs. Stafford-Jones prepare for the event.

At noon Clarence was given a rushed lunch, after which he escaped outside. He wandered about the garden raking up fallen twigs, snapping off the Jasmine creeper's wayward tentacles, and snipping off brown, curled Frangipani leaves. As the hours crept by, his nervousness turned to a sickly worry. As the shadows lengthened and darkness began to close in, he heard the front door open and watched the Stafford-Joneses leave in their car.

He ambled upstairs to find Ferna looking excited. She spoke quickly. "Hope ya don't mind Clarie if I don't ask ya to come with me, but tonight while I got the chance, me and Bill's goin' to go home to get some things I need. I'll be back before breakfast in the mornin'. I put ya tea in the oven. It's hot and ya can have it when ya ready."

"Thanks, but I'm not hungry. I'm going to bed early."

"I thought ya might be, you being an early-to-bed and early-to-rise bloke, but it's there for ya. See ya...'bye."

Now alone in the empty house, Clarence, with his soul filled with the odour of defeat, retreated to his room. He sank down on to his bed. "I'm doomed," he cried, as the old feeling of failure washed over him. Hours later when he turned off the bedside lamp and attempted to sleep, it was to no avail. Sleep had deserted him and he waited in despair for midnight and his expected journey to hell.

Suddenly, the sound of something being dropped made his eyes jerk open. He stayed tense, listening. Then out of the silence he heard footsteps on the garden path. Was it Ferna? No, she was not returning until the morning and it was too early for the Stafford-Joneses to be back.

He slid out of bed and peered out. A man's shadow fell across the path leading to the back door. A torch flashed on and off. *It must be a burglar.* He felt the cold hand of fear grip him. *What should I do?* Then the feeling turned to one of hope. *I'll ring the police...but how? I can't get into the house. He'll hear me.* He pondered the problem for a few moments than he remembered. *There's that public telephone not far down the road – I'll be doing the Stafford-Joneses a good turn. Perhaps providence is working with me at last.*

His slippers made no sound as he crept slowly, catlike, across the yard, blending himself with the dark shapes of the Oleanders. Then with a quick run across the open lawn he stood with his back against the trunk of a Magnolia tree and waited, listening. The only sound came from his beating heart. He moved on, losing a slipper as he climbed the low front fence. He did not stop to retrieve it. A truck was parked in front of the house, but he could see no one inside. Being cautious he crept from shadow to shadow along the footpath.

With shaking hands he telephoned the police station. In a breathless recital, he explained his dilemma to the policeman on duty. He was told to keep an eye on the burglar until they arrived. Clarence promised he would. After all, this was his last good deed.

He returned to the house, even more stealthily and felt no one could have spotted him. When reaching the back stairs a light was showing through the partly opened kitchen door. He crept, making no sound, up the steps. A voice reached him. *Ferna's?* He peered through the crack and spied a figure. It was Ferna. *Oh my...I've made a big mistake. That man must have been her Bill.* Clarence swung open the door. He gaped, his mouth fell open at the scene confronting him. Ferna was standing by the kitchen table putting Mrs. Stafford-Jones' silver into a garbage bag. Some shelves were already empty. She gave Clarence a fleeting glance but did not seem to notice the look of disbelief on his face. "Heard ya comin.' I knew it was ya. I was goin' to let ya in on it. It was Bill's idea, but ya such a Bible basher." She glanced at him again. "Ahh...don't get upset. Now ya here ya can help and we'll give ya a cop out of it."

"Ferna, please put everything back...please Ferna," he begged, but Ferna was only interested in collecting the gold plated cutlery and depositing it in the bag. "Please...." Clarence rung his hands as he searched for more persuasive words to use.

"Ahh, don't be stupid." Ferna said soothingly. "All this trouble for nothin? Not on ya life! Anyway no one'll suspect us. We'll be finished here before they get home. We'll say we was out, both of us together. Bill'll be our witness. Who's to know any different?" She walked to a glass cabinet and began to take down the antique china ornaments.

A man's voice made them both jump. It came from outside.

"The bloody cops...Scram!"

"That's me Bill's voice!" Ferna kicked away the half-filled bag, leapt over a packed box, pushed Clarence out of the way and disappeared down the stairs. Dumbfounded, Clarence stood gazing after her.

A policeman rushed into the room. "Got you red-handed. You're under arrest." The satisfied policeman raised his baton with one hand and pulled out his hand-cuffs with the other.

"B...but..." stuttered Clarence. "It wasn't me." He dutifully stretched out his arms and the policeman locked the handcuffs on his wrists.

"Explain it down at the police station," was the abrupt response.

A second policeman entered, escorting Ferna. She looked half asleep. Her hair was ruffled, and she was wearing a nightgown. Clarence gaped, his stomach twisting into a knot.

"I swear," she yawned. "I took a sleeping tablet...didn't hear nothin'."

"You know this man?"

"Sort of. It's like this officer. I never knew him 'till the other day when he gave me a hard luck story and I fell for it. Shows ya what can happen when ya does a good turn for somebody. Can I go now? I needs me sleep."

"Of course. We'll be in touch later today."

Ferna left, still ignoring Clarence.

Clarence was in a complete dreamlike state as he walked with the policeman to the police vehicle outside. He was pushed into the back seat and the door slammed shut as an urgent plea came from his companion somewhere in the darkest part of the garden.

"Give me a hand here Joe," was the breathless plea. "Got his accomplice with the goods and he's giving me trouble."

Clarence was sitting in the back seat, staring vacantly into space, when he suddenly felt a feeling of peace embrace him. Then everything dissolved into liquid, mixing and flowing together. He heard the constable who had returned, exclaim, "Now where's the blighter gone?"

Clarence felt himself free and floating upwards, to be joined by his two escorts. "What'll happen to me now?" moaned Clarence.

"Not for us to say." replied one.

Clarence, numb and now past worrying about what he believed was inevitable, soon found himself fronting the Guardian's desk, but it was a different Guardian.

"Welcome" said the silky voice of the new Guardian. "What is the name please?"

"Clarence Dudley," weakly replied Clarence.

"Angela, would you bring me Clarence Dudley's file please?"

Angela obliged.

"New arrival?" the Guardian queried.

No," said one escort. "Arrived a week ago today. He had to return to earth to do a last good deed."

"I can see that now...one moment. The name again?"
"Clarence Dudley."
"CLARENCE Dudley or DUDLEY Clarence?"
"Clarence Dudley."
"I can not believe it. That stupid relief of mine has mixed up the files again. Angela, Clarence Dudley's file please, NOT the Dudley Clarence one that fool requested you to bring to him." She floated off to return within seconds.

With the new file before him, the Guardian looked up at Clarence. "I am very sorry. You poor fellow, you should have been directed to Heaven immediately. That relief mixed you up with a Dudley Clarence, who might be called a bit of a backslider. I am sorry for the mistake. He should have checked and seen you were on Heaven's list of new entrants."

Clarence, who had been bracing himself in readiness to hear his sentence of an eternity of damnation or roasting in hell, slowly began to realize what had been said. "Mistake?" he hoarsely whispered

"Mistake?" echoed both escorts.

"Go now," ordered the Guardian smiling, "Someone is waiting for you."

'Waiting for me? My father?" Clarence's relief faltered, fearing that even in heaven he could not escape the domination of his father.

"No...a lady. And she has been waiting a long time."

"My mother perhaps?...or...or...could it be Kathleen?"

Relief and emerging joy at that possibility made Clarence laugh and cry, and cry and laugh. He was very noisy as they led him through the labyrinth of this new world towards the pearly gates of Heaven. Then he saw her. "Kathleen!" Kathleen, young and beautiful as he remembered her, was there waiting...waiting for him. His mother was forgotten.

Almost frozen with excitement, he almost stumbled as he ran forward. As he moved there was born a spring in his step. His body became lighter. His muscles tightened as his whole body changed. He too was young again.

Encircled by the waiting arms of his beloved Kathleen he knew he was definitely in Heaven. Hopefully his father – if here somewhere – would never find out Clarence had arrived.

Printed by Libri Plureos GmbH in Hamburg, Germany